GW00771681

A BRIDE FOR
SIR BERENGAR LE MOYNE

In 1258, seventeen-year-old Emma is faced with a dilemma: Her father is dying. He has sent for a comrade in arms, Sir Berengar le Moyne, to marry Emma if she agrees — and take her to his demesne of Bernewelle le Moyne, where she will be safe from the plots of her older half-brother Gerold, who plans to marry her to his only friend Sir Mauger when his father dies. Emma's eventual decision leads her into meeting King Henry III, his Queen, Eleanor of Provence, and Henry's son and his young bride, at the Royal Hunting Palace in Rockingham Forest.

DORA E. WOODHAMS

A BRIDE FOR
SIR BERENGAR LE MOYNE

Complete and Unabridged

ULVERSCROFT
Leicester

First published in Great Britain

First Large Print Edition
published 1999

British Library CIP Data

Woodhams, Dora
   A bride for Sir Berengar le Moyne.
   —Large print ed.—
   Ulverscroft large print series: romance
   1. Love stories
   2. Large type books
   I. Title
   823.9'14 [F]

   ISBN 0–7089–4066–8

Published by
F. A. Thorpe (Publishing) Ltd.
Anstey, Leicestershire
Set by Words & Graphics Ltd.
Anstey, Leicestershire
Printed and bound in Great Britain by
T. J. International Ltd., Padstow, Cornwall

This book is printed on acid-free paper

In loving memory of
George Frederick Woodhams
and of the enchanted land of
The Forest of Rockingham.

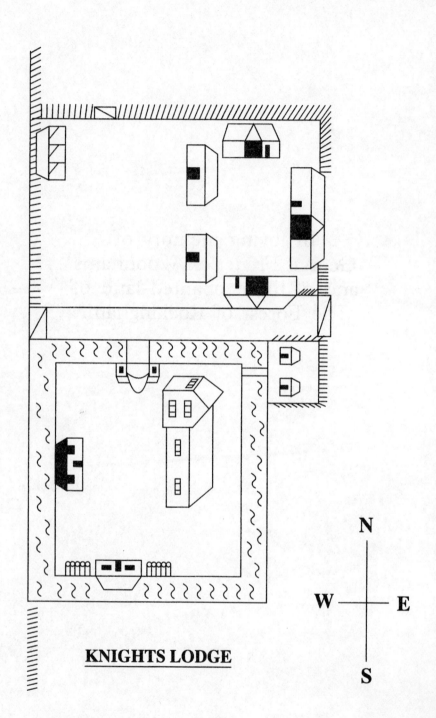

KNIGHTS LODGE

N

W   E

S

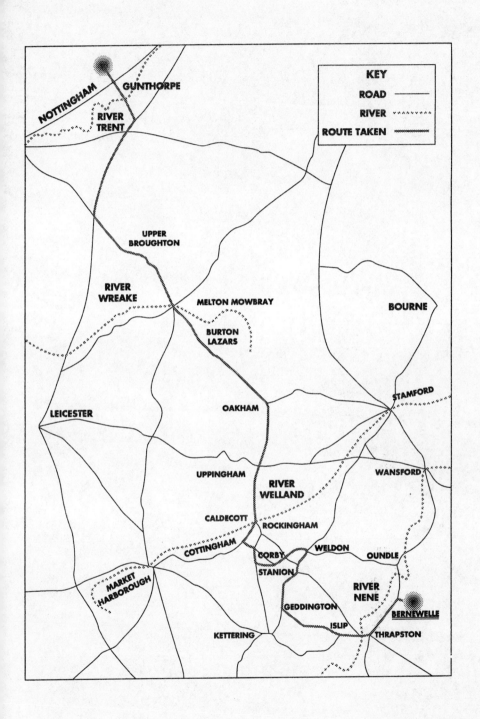

KEY
ROAD
RIVER
ROUTE TAKEN

NOTTINGHAM   GUNTHORPE

RIVER
TRENT

UPPER
BROUGHTON

RIVER
WREAKE

MELTON MOWBRAY

BURTON
LAZARS

BOURNE

OAKHAM

STAMFORD

LEICESTER

UPPINGHAM

RIVER
WELLAND

WANSFORD

CALDECOTT

ROCKINGHAM

COTTINGHAM

CORBY

WELDON

OUNDLE

STANION

RIVER
NENE

MARKET
HARBOROUGH

GEDDINGTON

BERNEWELLE

ISLIP

KETTERING

THRAPSTON

Historical Note

The stone walls of the castle which Sir Berengar le Moyne built at Bernewelle le Moyne in 1264 – 1266, still stand. (Barnwell today.) The earlier castle, probably of timber, was on the lozenge shaped mound (covered in small trees when I saw it) across the stream from the stone castle.

There *was* a great storm and flood along the East coast in the spring of 1258.

Knight's Lodge (North Lodge?) still stands, though the moat was filled in during the nineteen twenties.

Rockingham Castle and demesne still stand.

King Henry III is recorded as visiting Geddington Hunting Palace on August 26th, 27th, 28th, 29th, 30th and 31st, in 1258.

Most of the King's hawks were kept and trained in the mews at Geddington, — peregrines, goshawks, sparrowhawks, gerfalcons, merlins, kestrels and hobbies.

In 1267 Sir Berengar le Moyne was keeper of the peace in Huntingdonshire.

In 1270 Sir Berengar le Moyne was one of the collectors of the 20th, a tax levied on ecclesiastics and laity, in Huntingdonshire.

In 1270 Sir Berengar accompanied the Lord Edward (later King Edward I) on a crusade to Acre in the Holy Land.

Sir Berengar and Lady Emma le Moyne had two daughters, Rose (Roysia) and Margaret.

1

Emma stood in the chapel; her eyes fixed on the candle flame; her head held proudly; desolation in her heart.

The trails of incense, sweetly pungent, wreathed across the dimness.

Father Ailward's voice droned on; the candles flickered in the draught, flickered and burned steadily again, throwing dancing shadows across the altar cloth; the largest shadow being that of her destined husband, standing taut beside her.

Emma kept her gaze meekly lowered, and now fixed on her husband's hand — brown, scarred across the back with the white line of a spent dagger slash.

The fingers held hers strongly.

The priest's voice reached a climax. The man beside Emma repeated the Latin phrases — she knew the meaning well enough.

'I, Berengar, take thee, Emma, to my wedded wife, to have and to hold from this day forward, for better for worse, for richer for poorer, for fairer for fouler, in sickness and in health, till death us do part, if Holy Church it will ordain, and thereto I plight thee my troth.'

Emma's troth followed.

'I, Emma, take thee, Berengar, to my wedded husband, to have and to hold, from this day forward, for better, for worse, for richer for poorer, for fairer for fouler, in sickness and in health, to be meek and obedient in bed and at board till death us do part, if Holy Church it will ordain, and thereto I plight thee my troth.'

Sir Berengar placed a silver coin and gold trinket upon the Holy Book.

---------Creator et---------

Emma glanced sideways and tried to glimpse her father, lying prone on a stretcher that was steadied on trestles by his two oldest man servants.

Her attention was recalled.

'With this ring I thee wed and this gold and silver I thee give and with my body I thee worship and with all my worldly goods I thee endow.'

His fingers still held hers strongly. As his other hand slid the ring down upon her finger they retained their clasp.

Berengar felt Emma shiver, but he stood, imperturbable, smiling faintly — assured now of her lands and her body.

Well, she wished him joy of them.

Tears rose. Emma breathed more deeply and swallowed them. Her tears must be shed alone, not before this implacable soldier.

He knelt now beside her, concentration in his face. A face, tanned by sun and storm, hair bleached as pale as barley; the line from his helm marked round it like a cap.

The blood throbbed through his fingers and pounded against Emma's hand. She felt her robe brush against his sword scabbard as they rose. He freed it with one quick impatient movement.

Emma glanced up fleetingly, and read only haste in his face — no love, no pity, no concern, just impatience for the bond to be completed and the bride and her perquisites safely away with her lord and master.

His three men were in the bailey, the horses waiting, waiting for the bride to emerge, robed ready to ride with her lord and master, to do her new lord's bidding.

Was Emma ready? — Or was she going to try out her lord's temper?

He would expect obedience. Emma's fate was no worse than that of her contemporaries — a woman to be used as a pawn — a portion of your land here — my daughter brings you two manors — excellent, you accept, you need them urgently, they border your own?

'He must need them urgently to wed me,' thought Emma, 'A woman he saw for the first time today, his wedding day. The man the pedlar gossiped about four long years ago. The man who had finished with love and women at the ripe young age of eighteen. There would be no compassion in him for any woman.'

.... The blessing ....

It is the end — and the beginning.

Emma turned towards her father who was lying on a stretcher. She bent and kissed him, clutching his hand fervidly for a moment as he murmured, 'God take care of you.'

He knew what Emma was feeling, leaving him to a lingering death — and she knew that she must go.

He gave a slight pressure to her joined hands to open their clutch, then smiled contentedly up at her, as a man smiles who has accomplished a difficult task. Emma understood him, bent to kiss him again — and turned before tears triumphed.

Emma's Aunt Quenilda took both her hands in her own, then bent her tall aristocratic figure to hold Emma closely, kiss her, and whisper in her ear, 'I will

4

look after your father. Go quickly while you still have time.'

Emma resumed her place beside her husband. They paced sedately towards the open chapel door and the sunlight beyond.

It was August — good fighting weather for the Welsh wars. The intermittent wars were only carried on in spring and summer — winter was a time for attending to one's manor.

As they approached the open door to a new life, on this day, the twenty third day of August 1258, Emma's thoughts went back to almost a year ago — to the previous September when danger had insidiously crept into her life.

2

That September of 1257 had at first seemed like many others before it — just following the usual pattern of the farming year.

But one day Geva's footsteps had sounded on the steps up to the solar; hurried footsteps.

Geva had been tire woman to Emma's mother and was now her own maid.

Geva hurried through the doorway of the solar, bearing news.

'Lady Emma, your half brother, Sir Gerold has just ridden under the gatehouse arch and is dismounting in the bailey.'

The Lady Emma did not look enraptured over the news. Her half brother was older by five years and had mostly lived in the noble household where he had been sent as a young page to learn his duties — as page, then squire and finally knight.

'I expect, Geva, it is his duty to visit more often — now that he is twenty one, and of age, for he is after all my father's heir to the castle.'

'But he is not heir to your future dower lands,' replied Geva quickly. 'Those were your mother's dower, God rest her soul. They will be yours to bring to your husband when you marry.'

'When!' remarked Emma — 'I am seventeen already!'

'If only your mother had lived,' responded Geva sadly, 'I know that she had discussed your marriage. She told me that both she and your father wanted to wait a while until you were older and wiser — you were only twelve years old when the subject was mentioned. Your mother asked that you should meet any proposed bridegroom and approve of him before any contract was signed.'

Emma remembered her gracious mother, the Lady Isolda, as though her death had been yesterday, instead of three years ago.

Emma had been so happy until she had reached the age of fourteen — in spite of half brother Gerold, who never missed a chance of a quip at her expense.

'I must go down to the hall to welcome Sir Gerold,' Emma answered reluctantly, as she got up and put away her embroidery.

She walked quickly down the steps to the hall.

A tall, slim, elegant seventeen-year-old, dressed in a gown which fell in folds to her feet, and was laced up the back from the waist to the neck so that the gown clung to her closely, following every curve of her body and emphasising every movement.

Sir Gerold was talking to the Lady Quenilda, her father's sister, but as soon as he heard the whisper of her gown across the rushes covering the floor he turned, held out both hands to hold hers and kissed her cheek with great fervour.

'My small sister!' he enthused.

'No longer very small,' interrupted Lady Quenilda. 'Emma is now a young lady of seventeen years.'

'Then I must greet this young lady again,' and he lifted first one hand and then the other to kiss reverently.

A prickle of warning ran down Emma's spine.

'And where is my father?' Sir Gerold asked, apparently puzzled.

'He rests now, after noon, for two hours,' responded Lady Quenilda. 'You know that he was wounded in the Welsh war last year. It seemed a slight affair at the time. He was wearing armour; the blow fell on his knee cap; it seemed of little account. However by the time your father had arrived home from the war the bruises had faded but he still walked with a limp — which has got worse, not better.'

Gerold looked suitably concerned — but

there was a strange gleam of anticipation in his eyes.

The Lady Quenilda told Hanfrid, her brother's trusted man, to take Sir Gerold to him. She was frowning as Gerold disappeared from view.

'Now, I wonder,' she murmured to Emma, thoughtfully.

When they broke bread that evening, Sir Gerold watched his father with a calculating glance when he believed no one else was looking.

His manner was jovial. He made a point of talking to Emma on a subject he thought would interest her, though she gave him no encouragement.

'Lady,' he said, 'I wish you could have seen the King's latest toy — a present from the King of France, sent to amuse King Henry.

A strange animal, a tremendous, lumbering, grey animal, with ears like big flaps, and with a long tube coming out of its face. I saw the animal suck up water from a bucket through the tube and squirt it all over the man next to me.'

The Lady Quenilda quelled a wish that the animal had aimed a little farther on.

The Lady Emma responded, 'How interesting,' and sighed.

'I am going to fly my new tiercel peregrine tomorrow,' observed Gerold. 'Do come with me sister, I haven't talked with you for so long a time.'

Emma remembered the times without number when he had cold shouldered his young sister — and replied with a pensive expression, 'Very well, I will ride with you, if my aunt, the Lady Quenilda, will also ride with us.'

Sir Gerold looked nonplussed for a moment, then turned to the Lady Quenilda to beg her acceptance of his invitation.

Next morning Emma and her aunt rose with the sun, broke their fast on bread and water and were ready to ride early in the morning.

On departing through the main doorway beside her aunt, and entering the bailey, Emma saw Sir Gerold with a hooded, long winged peregrine upon the gloved left fist.

It was the male, the tiercel, a third smaller than a female peregrine. The hawk wore a bright red hood, covering the eyes. The hood had a tuft of feathers at the top and was fastened on by narrow leather straps, over the head and eyes of the bird. The tiercel had a bell attached to the leg above the jesses.

Osbert, the falconer stood, awaiting the

Lady Emma's arrival with her aunt.

The small company rode under the gatehouse arch and across the drawbridge until they reached the seamed and twisted ancient hawthorn tree which marked the edge of the common land. It grew upon a knoll and was the guardian of the meeting place of the hundred court.

Just now it was covered in haws, dark shiny red berries, in serried sprays along the branches.

Wild rose grew there too, with coral red hips, twice as large as the haws, and ending in a cap like calyx of five green pointed frills.

Blackberry bushes rampaged over the tussocks, throwing out snaking, springy shoots to overcurve the next patch of grass, and take root for more prickly invasions. White flowers were still star spotted among the sombre coloured brown-green-bronze-purple leaves, but the berry crop was good — each bush was covered in shining black, red and green 'pimpled' berries.

Growing up and entwining a seedling maple were tendrils of a winding plant that twined itself round and round along the low branches. All along the twisting bryony stem were luscious berries of a glowing, translucent scarlet, gem like in their intensity.

Beyond the bryony grew a tall plant with

succulent darker red berries. Here and there on it were tiny flowers, each made up of purple, pointed petals, forming a star round a centre of yellow — the woody nightshade.

Emma knew better than to nibble one of these fruits — or those of the black berried deadly nightshade.

Sir Gerold had by now finished his discussion with Osbert — who knew all the likely places where the tiercel would find prey when cast off.

The Lady Quenilda waited until Sir Gerold was busy striking the hood of his tiercel, casting loose his jesses and flying him at a wood pigeon, then quietly told Emma that she would come to speak with her in her portion of the solar, after Sir Gerold had retired to his bed that night.

All that morning Sir Gerold instructed Emma, with uncharacteristic patience, on the finer points in the art of falconry.

Osbert had to pull out the lure from his bag in order to retrieve the peregrine after he had made a kill.

Although it was a joy to be out in the sun and fresh breezes Emma was glad when Gerold turned for home.

His kind, patient, attentive care of her was worrying, unlike the Gerold she had known from childhood.

3

That night the Lady Quenilda softly entered the solar and crossed over to Emma's side of the room. She sat on the stool while Emma occupied the top of the wooden chest.

'This visit of Gerold's,' began the Lady Quenilda — 'I don't understand it. He knew about your father's wound last year, yet did not visit us. Has he mentioned a reason to you, child?'

'No,' replied Emma, 'And there is something odd in the way he behaves to me. He never bothered to notice my existence during the few visits he paid to his father before. Now he flatters me and apes the existence of a close companionship that has never, ever existed. He begs me to go with him when he flies his goshawk beside the stream tomorrow.'

'Fortunately he is only staying for a few days,' replied the Lady Quenilda.

'You don't like him either?' Emma questioned.

'No, nor trust him either,' continued her aunt. 'But then I knew his mother, the Lady Maud, your father's first wife. As a boy Gerold was very like his mother, very spiteful, very cunning.'

'Did not my father love his first wife, the Lady Maud?' asked Emma.

'Your father's first marriage was an arranged marriage. It was arranged by your grandfather and the father of the Lady Maud, before your father came of age. Your father hardly knew the Lady Maud at all, when he married. Unfortunately she was not a happy choice, and your father was locked in a loveless marriage bond. When it was over and the Lady Maud dead of a fever, your father's regret was for the manner of his wife's death. He was left with three-year-old Gerold, who resembled his mother. There — that is speaking plainly — but the time has come to speak plainly — for I fear that Gerold will bring trouble with him, now that he has realised that his father's health is failing. You must be on your guard, child. We can but wait and see. Gerold will have to show his hand eventually, whatever he is plotting. Now — to your bed. Later, when Gerold has left us I will speak with your father.'

It was with a sigh of relief that Emma bade 'Farewell' to Sir Gerold as he rode back to his duties.

Emma could return to her interests in the manor.

The threshing was nearly finished. Sounds of much flailing activity had been coming from the barn for many days.

October went by quickly. The cider had been fermented, the oil pressed from the gathered nuts, the honey taken from the hives.

At this time the swineherd took his herd of swine into the woods to find wild pears, plums, crab apples, sloes, haws and acorns which had fallen from the trees.

During November came the salting of pork and beef.

After the harvest the hayward removed the fences and the animals were allowed on the land to feed on the left overs of the harvest.

The best cattle and pigs were kept for breeding next year but the rest were slaughtered.

December brought a message from Sir Gerold. The messenger announced that Sir Gerold and a friend would be coming to spend Christmas with Sir Gerold's father.

They arrived on the Eve of Christmas, stamping their feet to get the feeling back after the cold journey. Sullen grey clouds had hung heavy in the sky all day.

Remaining very quietly by the side of the Lady Quenilda as she welcomed Sir Gerold and his friend, Sir Mauger, Emma escaped as soon as she could to the solar.

Her father limped so badly now that he had to heave himself along by the aid of two sticks of ash wood.

After the evening breaking of bread Sir Gerold and Sir Mauger played at chess on the chequered board.

Gerold realised with something of a jolt that his young half-sister was no longer a child, but a woman, and a very beautiful young woman, tall, lithe, slim, with delicious curves, and long, curling dark hair.

Gerold began to weave plans for the future. He doubted that his father would live beyond the next year.

Once he became unable to walk at all and had to lie prone in bed the chest inflammation would attack him — and for that there was no cure.

Then he, Gerold, would be the new Lord of the Manor.

He decided to be exceedingly affable to Emma.

4

Christmas Day dawned with a fitful flickering white light.

Emelota opened the wooden shutters of the narrow slit window in Emma's portion of the solar. Then she almost closed them.

A drift of snowflakes swirled into the room. Myriads of small white flakes were falling outside. There was already a white sprinkling of snow covering the bailey and the roof of the gatehouse.

Emma dressed quickly.

The throng of villeins would arrive early for the noon day meal — the reeve, hayward, carter, head reaper, miller, warrener, shepherd, cowherd, falconer, granger, huntsman, ploughman, oxherd, ale wife, poultry woman, among them.

The men and women of the household, who slept in the hall, were up and already at work.

Logs were being dragged in to pile on the hot embers of the fire on the paving stones, which made an octagonal hearth in the centre of the hall.

The trestle tables were being erected, with

benches placed behind them.

The high table, on its dais at the end of the hall, was covered by a linen cloth: the flanking tables had bare wooden boards.

An hour before noon Emma's father took up his position in the hall, as Lord of the Manor, to welcome his freemen, his villeins and bordars.

They came cloaked and hooded against the swirling snow, faces frozen by braving a biting wind; turning at once towards the blazing logs for the forked flames to thaw them out.

As the hall filled, the steam rose from dozens of damp woollen tunics and hose.

Noon approached. Everyone took his or her place at the board.

Emma's father stood by his central seat at the high table, with the Lady Quenilda, Emma, Sir Gerold, Sir Mauger and Father Ailward.

Father Ailward pronounced the prayers, Emma's father sat down; all followed suit.

There was a hush of expectancy.

A swirl of cold air came round the draught spur at the far end of the hall — then everyone could see two men carrying a large serving dish on which was the boar's head, with tusks, and an apple in its mouth, fresh from the kitchen outside.

18

The serving men and wenches followed the boar's head. Each man or maid carried a platter of roast meats.

A trencher for each reveller lay upon the board; each had brought his own knife with which to cut his meat.

Freemen were given a whole hen between two, with roast meat for the second course, and cheese, and ale.

Everything was going smoothly.

Emma lapsed into a haze of contentment, idly watching the familiar figures she had known since childhood, as she ate — noting the ripples of laughter from this group or that.

Tostan, a serving lad, was pouring wine for Sir Mauger. Tostan was about twelve years of age, slender as a girl, fair haired, fair skinned, with cheeks delicately tinged with roseate colour.

Still idly following movement here and there Emma saw Sir Mauger's gaze become fixed on the youth pouring the wine, beside him. His nostrils flared, his hand clenched.

A dribble of wine had flecked Sir Mauger's sleeve. His hand grasped the boy's wrist, crushing the flesh against the bone. Sir Mauger's face gloated over the pain he was causing.

'Back to the buttery,' ordered Emma's father quickly.

A chill swept over Emma.

At a signal from her father a jongleur came forward into the centre space.

First he sang carols — 'The Boar's head in hand bring I' and 'Nowell,' among them.

When the dancing began Emma hoped that she would be able to remain sitting beside her father. He was frowning and looking somewhat grim.

He did not urge Emma to take part in the dancing — but Gerold took her hand most deferentially.

'I beg you sister, to take part with me.'

Emma looked at her aunt, who gave a tiny, unsmiling nod.

As she was returning to her father's side, after the strumming and singing ceased she found Sir Mauger barring the way, bowing and laughingly asking Sir Gerold for his partner's hand.

Sir Gerold gave Emma's hand into Sir Mauger's clasp, and he led her back to the dance.

The singing again emphasised the beat of the rhythm.

As Emma danced she kept as far as possible away from Sir Mauger. She gauged him to be older than Gerold, experienced in war, but not only in war.

She saw a man of middle height, dark

haired and oily complexioned, with small pits in the skin of his face. His fleshy lips smiled fulsomely but his eyes were cold with calculation.

Emma played her part too — not always perfectly — sometimes the smile slipped a little.

As on the day after Christmas. Emma was hurrying into the pentice covered way joining the hall to the kitchen outside, when she came upon Sir Mauger unexpectedly.

He had pinned the fair haired serving lad, Tostan, against a roof support. The lad had struggled to escape. Sir Mauger was twisting the youth's arm slowly and with great deliberation, forcing him to beg for mercy.

The expression on Sir Mauger's face was one of gloating pleasure at the pain he was inflicting.

Then he sensed Emma's presence, glanced up, and let the boy go, his face changing, shrugging as he did so.

'A clumsy lout — he nearly tripped me,' he complained.

Emma began counting the days to the New Year, to the day of Sir Mauger's departure.

The longed for day came at last. Sir Gerold and Sir Mauger left, to travel to Sir Mauger's demesne.

21

The following morning the Lady Quenilda came to Emma as she was waking.

She sat up in bed looking questioningly at her aunt.

'I have spoken to your father again, and have warned him that I believe that Gerold has some devious plan in mind. He is convinced that Gerold is visiting the castle more often because he is of age and for no other reason.'

'What of Sir Mauger?' asked Emma.

'Your father does disapprove strongly of Sir Gerold's friendship with Sir Mauger — and thinks him a bad influence on his son. But he is confident that Gerold will find this out for himself.'

Emma and the Lady Quenilda smiled wryly at each other.

'I cannot find it in my heart to tell your father that he is much worse. He thinks that he will get well again. But I have seen this creeping palsy before. After quite a small blow or accident it can attack the strongest of men — or women.'

'You think there is no hope?'

'None, though he has some months left to him.'

'Months? — Not years?'

'I fear — only months.'

Emma could not envisage life without her

father, and tears rolled down her cheeks.

'I will help you in every way I can,' comforted the Lady Quenilda, 'But until your father sees for himself that Gerold means mischief, he will continue to believe that you will be as safe under Gerold's protection as under his own.'

5

A few days after Sir Mauger's departure snow came again.

The flakes were larger. They eddied down unceasingly and with such blinding force that it was hard to make one's way against the white whorls.

Cloaked and hooded Emma leaned against the power of the swirling whiteness and forced her way to the gatehouse to view the vista towards the hamlet, fields and woods.

The snow lay six inches deep already, after a night's fall. If there should be no lifting of the leaden sky the snow would be a foot deep by nightfall.

Each homestead had its white headdress. Every tree was transfigured, etched in sparkling white softness, blurring the outlines of the leafless trees, blanketing in drifts of crisp whiteness the yew and holly.

Whiteness stretched in front of Emma, across the land, until it merged into the eddying whiteness descending from above.

There was no horizon. It was completely blotted out.

The shepherd had a hard time of it.

Fortunately the thatched, moveable shelters protected most of the sheep from being buried in the snow. They huddled against the shelter of the fold as snow drifted in the fields.

But by Candlemas, February 2nd, the last of the snow had melted.

In the chapel Father Ailward handed Emma a candle, which she kissed. It was lighted from the neighbouring candle and remained alight throughout the mass.

The yellow, scaly stemmed coltsfoot was alight too, pushing up through the sodden ground beside the ditch. Opening its yellow rayed petals to the weak sunlight it reminded Emma of the promise of its cousin, the summer's dandelion.

In March the oats were sown.

In April the fallow field was ploughed.

One night in Spring there was a storm of high winds and rain.

Emma woke and listened. Everywhere was dark, but there was a distant sound of whining which increased in volume until it was a howl.

The wind was steadily gaining in force so that the wooden shutters rattled and shook with the strength of the gale.

Huddled under the bed covers Emma heard a frightening creaking sound and then a rending crash from outside.

25

Suddenly the power of the roaring wind forced the shutters apart, tore them from their hinges and flung them across the room.

Emma's Aunt Quenilda cried out to her, 'Child, are you hurt?'

'No,' replied Emma, 'But I'm coming across to you. We must find a safer place to wait for the storm to die down.'

Emma clawed her way out of bed, clutched her cloak by the light of a lightning flash, felt her way across the room to her aunt's bedside.

Holding hands Emma guided her aunt across the floor to the open doorway with the wind sweeping through it.

Once through the doorway the two women felt their way along the wall and nearly bumped into Radulf and Hanfrid who were guiding Emma's father to the top of the steps to the great hall where the men and maids huddled together as the lightning flashed.

Radulf lit the rush lights.

Emma's father gave orders for everyone to stay in the hall until the gale died down.

The shrieking wind lasted all night, punctuated by the smashing of tiles into the courtyard and the splintering of trees in the distance.

When the faint grey light of dawn came from the East the storm still raged, but as the morning wore on the frighteningly strong gusts of wind blew less often and by twelve noon had begun to lose their strength.

The men were able to go out to ascertain the immediate damage.

They returned to report that the giant oak at the end of the forest lay on the ground, its roots pathetically pointing skywards, eight feet in the air, thicker than a man's arm. Where the roots had anchored the ancient tree was a large crater.

Tiles littered the courtyard.

The moveable sheep folds looked as though they had been picked up by a giant's hand, then smashed against the hedgerow.

Fences had been torn up, blown away, and eddied into heaps of splintered wood.

Hanfrid and three men went to the village. They gathered as much news as they could.

The oxherd had dragged his wife from under a tree that had crashed on to his house, fortunately across a corner. The opposite corner had held firm long enough to get the woman out.

Many outbuildings in the village had collapsed into rubble.

Emma helped her father to tally the damage, both to the castle and the demesne.

Everyone gathered round to listen as the news came in.

Hanfrid was sent on a journey to Gunthorpe by the Trent river to see if he could pick up news from further afield.

Three days later he came into the hall guiding a draggled figure who carried a bundle tied up in a cloth.

Hanfrid halted the traveller in front of Emma, her aunt, and her father.

'A man from King's Lynn, Messire, by the name of Alfric. He brings news.'

'My Lord,' began Alfric, 'I am lucky to be alive when so many in King's Lynn drowned in the great storm. It was a terrible night. A raging gale of wind forced a surge of the high tide. The townsmen later put a mark on the sea wall. The tide was eight feet higher than it should have been. It surged over the sea walls and flooded the town. In the darkness many people had no chance to climb on to the roofs to save themselves. They were swept away on the flood water and drowned. I was lucky. I was visiting my brother-in-law whose house is two stories high. We were able to climb to the loft floor level and we stayed there until daylight. In the afternoon a man in a rowing boat saw us waving, came to the rescue, and rowed us to dry land. Bodies of men, women and children floated in the sluggish waters. Sheep and cattle had drowned as the sea and river waters overflowed into the fields. There was one vast expanse of water, marked here and there by a line of hedgerow tree tops where the field boundaries had once been.'

Alfric was rewarded for his news and taken away to be given food, fresh clothing and a bed for the night.

Hanfrid returned next day to Gunthorpe. Two days later he returned from Gunthorpe with another traveller, one named Edric, also from the East Coast.

Hanfrid brought him to Emma and the Lady Quenilda.

'Edric journeys to Southwell, my lady,' reported Hanfrid. 'He survived the storm and bears messages to the provost.'

Edric spread out his hands. 'Where can I begin, lady? We were not expecting a great storm. The fishing boats were at anchor in the harbour as usual as the sun went down. By next morning the boats had been lifted by the storm surge, swept on to the land and smashed into splinters. Bridges had been swept away, houses had collapsed into the waters. It is a great disaster. Even the old men cannot remember a storm as dreadful as this one. Nearly all the East Coast sea defences have been breached. The land is flooded in Lincolnshire, Huntingdon, Norfolk and Suffolk and Cambridgeshire.'

Edric was rewarded and given food, clothing and a bed for the night before he continued his journey next day.

6

Many weeks after the news of the great flood on the East Coast became known throughout the land Gerold came riding under the gatehouse arch and into the bailey.

He was paying a visit to his father before returning to the borders of Wales to the Welsh war.

What he saw in his father's sunken face made him seek out Emma, where she was gathering sprigs from the herb garden to make a sweet smelling posy to put in her father's room.

'Well met, little sister. I cannot stay long, but long enough to congratulate you on your conquest.'

'I know of no conquest brother,' replied Emma quickly.

'Ah, such modesty becomes you,' purred Gerold, 'But surely you noted at the Christmas revels how much Sir Mauger admired you. He offers for your hand in marriage.'

The revulsion showed in Emma's face.

Sir Gerold leered speculatively.

'You do not like him?'

31

Emma's face set like a mask. 'No.'

'Let me point out that at our father's death your marriage will be at my bidding — you will marry who I command you to marry.'

Silence followed, the silence of refusal.

Sir Gerold sneered, 'You may refuse consent — as many others have likewise refused consent, to the choice of their brothers or fathers. They are married to that choice today, as will you do likewise.'

Emma looked steadily at him and shook her head. 'No.'

He reddened. 'Ay, you can speak words of refusal. Of what avail will that be to you? — When Sir Mauger's ardour has got the better of him and he has deflowered you. You will marry him fast enough then, I warrant — and glad to do so.'

Emma buried her face in her posy of green herbs so that Gerold could not see it.

Her quick ears had caught a slight sound behind the herb garden's thick evergreen hedge.

As Gerold pointed out, it was of course quite a common practice. A recalcitrant girl refused to marry the man of her family's choice for her.

First a beating into submission would be tried. If that failed then events were arranged accordingly.

The law forbade the covering of an unwilling woman — but there were always plenty to swear, for a consideration, that the woman had been willing.

When she possessed lands she became a pawn in a game of chess.

Emma intended to try her best to provide checkmate to Gerold's little game.

Sir Gerold's last words were hissed in a cutting voice, 'You are just like your mother, the Lady Isolda. She bewitched my father; he worshipped at her feet — but you, you bitch — you won't be able to bewitch Sir Mauger, will you? He's after your lands — for which I get some recompense too — he'll make sure he's cowed you before he throws you aside for his latest fancy.'

With that Gerold turned on his heel, strode angrily back to the bailey, called for his horses and men, and departed for the Welsh war.

Emma trod slowly back to the hall, still holding her posy of herbs.

She saw Hanfrid hurrying into the buttery, then returning with a cup of wine in his hand, but she climbed the steps up to the solar, so completely lost in thought that she did not question Hanfrid.

Emma was sitting with her embroidery in her hands, staring into space, with her needle poised in her hand, when Emelota, her old nurse (and now the Lady Quenilda's maid), came up to her.

'Lady Emma, your father wants to speak to you in his room.'

Emelota captured Emma's attention.

Emma put down her embroidery, stood, and followed Emelota to her father's room.

He was sitting in a high backed chair. Hanfrid was holding another wine cup to his lips, for him to drink the wine.

Radulf was picking up the two walking sticks which had dropped on to the floor, and the Lady Quenilda was wrapping a wool coverlet over her brother's feeble frame.

'Hanfrid, Radulf, leave me until I call,' commanded Emma's father.

Emma ran to her father and held one of his hands between hers.

'What has happened? What has made you so white and ill?'

Her father was breathing more easily now and some colour was returning to his face.

'Tell her, my lady,' he said to the Lady Quenilda.

'God forgive me,' replied Lady Quenilda. 'When Sir Gerold went in search of you, Emma, I begged your father to go with me to the path behind the hedge that surrounds the herb garden. I told him that it was most important that he should hear what Gerold said to you. Hanfrid and Radulf half carried your father there and he stood, supported by his two walking sticks and two retainers, behind the dense hedge all the time Gerold was speaking to you.'

'My child,' began Emma's father, 'You must have realised that I have not long to live.'

Emma slowly nodded her head.

'My death,' went on her father, 'will leave you in the sole power of Sir Gerold, and he will then have the disposal of your hand (and lands) in marriage. Until this day I believed that Sir Gerold would protect you and carry out my wishes when I was laid to rest. What I heard today from Sir Gerold has been a tremendous shock to me. I have little time left but I must and will right the wrong I have done you. I should have made sure soon after I was wounded, that you were suitably married, with a husband to protect you. The resulting illness came upon me so slowly that I deemed there was still time, that I would have many years left to protect you and find an acceptable husband to make you happy. You will, on your marriage, hold the dower lands which your mother brought to me when I married her, though I married your mother for love, not the lands she brought.'

Emma remembered the happy years she had spent as a child; remembered her gracious mother the Lady Isolda, who never raised her voice, yet was obeyed by all the inmates of the castle.

The Lady Quenilda smiled faintly.

'Your father remarried after the death of Sir Gerold's mother, this time a lady of his own choice, for by now he was of age, and his father was dead. You were born a year after your father wedded the Lady Isolda. My husband and I saw you, on our yearly visits, watched you grow from a baby to an elegant, dark haired young girl.'

The Lady Quenilda sighed. 'Then my husband was killed in the Welsh wars and I became resident in an abbey — retiring from the world, but not taking vows. Gerold was placed in the household of Sir Giffard de Tours to train as page, then squire, and eventually knight.'

Emma's father spoke with great feeling. 'Your mother and I discussed your future marriage Emma. Our own happiness made us wish to arrange a marriage for you with your consent — and approval. Your mother, when you first reached marriageable age, wanted to wait a while until you were older and wiser — and stipulated that you must meet the proposed bridegroom a number of times

36

before any contract was approved.'

Emma well remembered this blissful state continuing until she was fourteen. She looked at her father. 'You both hoped for a son, did you not?'

'Just so. In your fourteenth year, your mother, who was loved and wanted so much, was again with child, but as you know — at the eighth month the Lady Isolda tripped and fell awkwardly. The babe was born straightway, dead, and your mother died two hours later.'

The wasted hands gripped at the coverlet with the agony of remembrance.

'Child, you tried to help me, but indeed you were so like your mother that sometimes you did not realise that just to look at you made my loss the greater. I needed a chaperone for you, and someone to manage the affairs of the manor while I was away on knight service with the King's army. I persuaded your aunt, the Lady Quenilda to leave the abbey, where she was living a secluded life, and to come here to be châtelaine of the castle. You know what happened later?'

Yes, Emma knew what happened later — only too well.

'Now,' said her father, grimly, 'I must live long enough to see you safely married to one who can protect you from Sir Gerold and Sir Mauger.'

Emma gasped and looked first at her father and then at Lady Quenilda.

'No,' said her father, 'I am not going to tell you more just now. Suffice it to say that such a person exists, though exactly where he is at this moment, I am not sure. Therein lies the danger. I must send Hanfrid and Radulf as my trusted messengers. One messenger needs must go to the Welsh Marches where also is Sir Gerold. Sir Gerold is not a fool. I will tell you more, and certainly you will be able to view your proposed rescuer, and make up your own mind about him when my messengers return.'

Emma kissed her father's sunken cheek and at a nod from her aunt went back to her embroidery, with her mind in a turmoil.

Who could this young man be? Why was her father so sure of him?

As soon as Geva came through the doorway, bringing in a pile of fresh linen, Emma questioned her.

'Have you heard of any unwed knight living within thirty miles of here?'

'No,' replied Geva, looking puzzled.

'Promise you will keep this a secret,' urged Emma.

'I promise,' vowed Geva.

'Then Geva,' begged Emma, 'Think hard. My father has spoken of one who may be a prospective bridegroom for me. Is there anyone who could have visited the castle without my knowing?'

'No,' replied Geva. 'But there is that ungodly Sir Mauger who came last Christmas. Surely your father does not mean to give your hand in marriage to that one.'

'No, I know that he does not mean Sir Mauger, thanks be to God,' returned Emma.

Geva brightened as she thought of an idea. 'Perhaps he is thinking of a widower, one who is looking for a lady to be a mother to his children.'

'Yes, there is that answer,' replied Emma without noticeable enthusiasm. 'Such a one would certainly be able to protect me. Thank you, Geva, you have given me something to think about.'

Emma's thoughts about someone probably as old as her father did not noticeably improve her spirits.

The Lady Quenilda had no further news except that Hanfrid and Radulf had both left the castle bearing a message.

Emma's father grew increasingly weak and increasingly worried.

7

The months of that year 1258 had gone by so quickly.

No sooner did the grass of the hay plots grow to six inches high, a succulent green, than quickly it was a foot high, then ready for the scythes of the mowers in June.

No sooner was the hay stacked than preparations began for the grain harvest.

The reaping was done with a sickle. Rye and wheat were reaped.

Early one morning in August hoofs clattered to a standstill at the gatehouse, and four men then rode under the gatehouse arch and into the bailey.

Emma went with her aunt to the great main door of the castle, as was the courtesy custom to receive a visitor.

The leader swung down lithely from the saddle and announced himself as Sir Berengar le Moyne.

Emma was left somewhat breathless (for she had suddenly remembered the chapman's story from four years ago).

She looked up at a tall, rangily built man, loose limbed, broad shouldered, with

40

the habit of command.

He commanded now, though it was politely phrased enough.

He was welcomed by the Lady Quenilda and the Lady Emma, but he stated at once that his business was with Emma's father.

His glance swept over Emma as he made the request. His face remained without expression but Emma had the feeling that he had noted everything about her, from the topmost tendril of dark hair, to the soft leather shoes on her feet.

As Sir Berengar strode off, with Engret as guide to take him to Emma's father, her glance followed the tall, straight figure.

Remembering the tale of the beautiful Diote, Emma wondered if she had ever regretted tossing aside the illusion and grasping the reality in the shape of a solid, if unexciting husband.

Emma smiled thoughtfully. Not that Sir Berengar looked especially romantic — vibrant, and energetic maybe, but completely controlled.

The two men were closeted together for an hour.

Then Engret came back to conduct Sir Berengar to the hall to partake of refreshment.

Emma went to her father.

He was lying in his bed, which he could by now seldom leave. He held out his hand to her.

'Child,' he said, quietly. 'Listen to me. I am desirous of settling your future before I die. This is *not* the way I would have planned your betrothal had I had longer to live. You should know that I have been acquainted with Sir Berengar le Moyne for some years now — indeed I saved his life when he was but a squire in '54. He needs a wife. We spoke of you, child, some years ago.'

Emma looked the question, 'Why?'

'After I saved young Berengar's life he went in the early summer on leave from the Welsh border to his home at Bernewelle le Moyne. He went home rejoicing in his deliverance, confident, full of quips and merriment, jocularly referring to me as his father preserver. He returned to the camp a young man of a different stamp, morose, bitter, cynical, careless of the life I had preserved for him. Not willing to see him needlessly sacrificed I spoke to him as a father would have done; my first intervention in saving his life having given me some right. I do not propose to burden you with the details of his disclosures.'

(Here Emma looked disappointed.)

'I will just say that young Berengar had

lost all faith in a woman's word, deemed all women fickle, had abandoned all thought of marriage, which was his eventual duty when he came of age, for his father had been dead for some years. We talked well into the night. He gave his word that if I ever needed his help he would come to my aid. He cared not who he wed. Now I have asked for his help. Sir Berengar is willing to wed you at once.'

Emma gasped. Her father glanced down for a moment. A word of explanation seemed necessary.

'He will be glad of the collateral of your dower lands, before he can rebuild at Bernewelle le Moyne.'

Here Emma swallowed a tart reply.

Her father went on, 'I sent my messenger secretly to tell Sir Berengar of my severe illness and your imminent peril at the hands of Sir Gerold.

Sir Berengar is willing for marriage at once — but are you willing child?'

Emma looked dumbly at her father. Thoughts jostled each other. No, she was not willing to be handed over summarily to this haughty, and dusty, stranger. One who moreover had vowed to eschew women.

She went to the slit window and stood looking out, seeing, not the bailey in front of her but a tall, straight, grim figure, hard grey eyes, the wary glance of a man armed against the wiles of women.

But he looked fastidious, very unlike the oily Sir Mauger.

The mental picture of Sir Mauger twisting the serving boy's arm returned. Only her father's life stood in the way of a far worse fate for her.

Emma's father spoke again. 'Gerold must have already noticed that Sir Berengar has not taken his allotted part in the Welsh war — for the King's command to muster for war in Wales came to the shires some time ago. It was dated for the 28th day of December 1257, in the last month of last year. At Broughton, in April, Sir Berengar was chosen to be one of the four knights to go to the Welsh war on behalf of the Abbot of Ramsey. Afterwards another knight went in his place. You are lucky, for though Sir Berengar had been chosen for knight service in Wales he was prevented from performing that service. Sheer chance intervened, in the shape of the great sea flood this spring. Sir Berengar has lands in Huntingdonshire, Cambridgeshire and Northamptonshire, and he was required to survey the flooding there and report to the King's representative, Henry de Bathe. So the innundation survey took precedence over the knight service — for another Knight of the Abbey could be found to perform that duty. I sent two messengers to find Sir Berengar, Hanfrid to Bernewelle le Moyne and Radulf to the army's camp on the Welsh Marches. Both messengers carried identical pleas — asking Sir Berengar's help in protecting you, and informing him of my serious illness. Radulf has reported back that one of Sir Gerold's men saw him at the camp and is sure to inform Gerold of this. Hanfrid found Sir Berengar at Bernewelle le Moyne. He had just returned from an inspection of the rebuilt dyke walls. He set off at once to accompany Hanfrid and ride here. He has only three of his men with him — for he rode in haste to reach us. By now Gerold will have been asking questions in the camp and will have heard that Radulf was enquiring for Sir Berengar. Gerold is not a fool. He will probably guess what is afoot, gain permission for leave from the camp and come to investigate. If you wish to be rescued from Sir Mauger you must make up your mind quickly. If you are willing, then the marriage will take place in an hour's time and you must ride with haste to Bernewelle le Moyne. There your husband can protect you within his castle palisade.'

The mental picture of Sir Mauger arose

again in front of Emma.

She shuddered — and decided.

'I will wed, father — but what of you when I am gone?'

'I shall do well enough child — your aunt the Lady Quenilda will stay here as long as Gerold will allow her to remain. Radulf will stay beside me and Emelota, your old nurse will be at hand. One thing more. Your future husband has given me his word that the bedding will take place when you reach Bernewelle le Moyne. You will have three days at least to find out how to please him.'

Emma's father smiled weakly at his joke.

'Father — you are sure you wish for this?'

'Yes, child, there is great hope for your safety and happiness once wedded to Sir Berengar.'

Emma's father summoned Hanfrid to go and fetch Sir Berengar — who strode over to the bed, his face impassive, and stood looking down at Emma's father.

Emma felt panic rising. Her father called her name; she trod over to the bed to stand beside Sir Berengar. Her father took her hand and placed it palm down on Sir Berengar's upturned palm.

At once his other hand closed over it so

46

that it was engulfed completely and Emma's father could not see that her hand was trembling.

Her father gave his blessing to the couple in front of him.

As his voice dropped Emma looked quickly up through her lashes at the face above hers. The grey eyes met her glance but they were unreadable.

There was no warm look of admiration in them such as she was accustomed to seeing in a man's glance.

'Lady,' he said quietly, 'I pledge myself to your protection.'

Well, Emma supposed it was fair exchange — his protection for her lands.

The small matter of love remained unremarked.

8

An hour is not long for preparation for a wedding.

Two kitchen wenches were sent scurrying to fetch the wooden bath tub. They fetched pitcher after pitcher of hot and cold water from the kitchen, and gradually half filled it.

The Lady Quenilda directed the packing of saddle bags.

'Careful, girl, keep the pleats in that linen shift as you fold it,' to Geva. 'Here, Emelota, hand the Lady Emma this silk shift.'

Emma had bathed quickly in lukewarm water and was now rubbed dry with the linen towel until she was tingling all over.

She slid the shift over her head and smoothed it down over her slim hips. The undergown followed it.

The good gown of light blue went next over her head.

Geva laced it up the back, from the hips upwards to the finishing knot at the neck, so that it fitted the curves of Emma's figure exactly. The gown's skirt fell in full folds to the floor. The neckline was rounded, and slit, banded with embroidery.

'Come Geva, hurry, comb the Lady Emma's hair,' commanded the Lady Quenilda.

Left loose, it curled duskily to Emma's thighs.

She knew that after the wedding and their arrival at Bernewelle le Moyne two plaits would be coiled round her ears, and she would assume the married woman's head dress — the barbette — a linen band passing under the chin up to a white circlet of linen round the head.

Emelota was hurriedly packing a saddle bag, folding Emma's best and only other gown of light greenish blue watchet, ready for when she arrived at Bernewelle le Moyne.

'What happened to your mother's gowns?' Aunt Quenilda was frowning with concentration.

'They are still in the chest, where they were put after she died,' Emma replied, puzzled.

Her aunt looked her up and down.

'You look to me, now you have grown to be nearly eighteen, to be much of your mother's size. Give Geva the key to the chest and bid her bring the contents here, a few at a time.'

Geva came back, securely holding a bundle, sewn up in linen wrappings.

After carefully unpicking the stitches of

the covering linen Geva held up a tawny coloured gown with yellow embroidery at the neck.

Emelota unpicked the covering linen from the second bundle and held up a gown of red embroidered in turquoise blue.

Emma and the Lady Quenilda looked at them closely — even two years ago they would have been too large for Emma — now they looked just right.

Lady Quenilda nodded for the two gowns to be packed with the others.

Hurrying, Emma pulled on her short hose to the knee, tied the garters just below the knee, and slipped her feet into pointed, soft leather shoes, each with a strap.

The preparations and packing finished, there remained just the wedding itself. Then Emma would be galloping away to (what she hoped was) safety.

9

As Emma and her newly wedded husband
emerged from the shadow of the chapel into
the full sunlight of the bailey there was a
flurry of excited movement.

Nearly everyone concerned with the
kitchen, stable, brewhouse and bakehouse
had assembled to view the departure of the
bride and her husband.

Geva quickly slung Emma's cloak round
her shoulders and fastened the corner through
the brooch hasp on her shoulder.

Emma's husband lifted her to her saddle
— a wave — and they were off to a new (and
for Emma, a possibly forbidding) future.

As the horses trotted beneath the arch of
the gatehouse Emma looked towards her
childhood's fascination — the dog court.

There by the wood slatted entrance stood
her childhood's ally — Leofric — now a
young man of fourteen years — huntsman
— no longer the humble dog boy whose duty
it was to sleep in the kennel to ensure the
good behaviour and safety of the hounds.

He stood, clothed in the knee length tunic
of russet wool, the waist pouched over a

belt and showing the marked fold of the undergarment beneath.

His cowled hood was pushed back and hung down his back, its lirapipe reaching to the hem of the tunic.

His hose were wrinkled as though they had been pulled up in a hurry, the points tied too loosely to the waist cord for a good fit. He wore short pointed-toed boots and held his master's favourite lymer on his rope of well tawed leather.

Emma had never minded the smell of dog piss as long as she was allowed to be taken by her nurse to visit the kennel and to see the whelps.

She remembered as a fascinated five-year-old being on hands and knees, comforting a whelp. It had been separated from the bitch and was confined in a barrel that lay on its side. The whelp was peering through the slats across the open end of the barrel, and whining piteously.

She remembered her twelve-year-old self who forgot her newly acquired dignity once (accompanied by Emelota) she was through the slatted gate and talking of hounds and whelps with Wandril and Leofric.

Most of all she remembered one particular day when she was nearly fourteen.

Emma's mother had taught her all she

knew of herbs and simples.

The treatment of a sick hound was in essence similar to the treatment of a sick man.

Her father was away at the Welsh war.

The Lady Isolda stood up at the end of the mid-day meal in the great hall. Emma now had a place beside her, at the centre of the trestle table. (Two more tables were placed down the length of the hall from either end of the high table on its dais, at right angles to it.)

All who worked at the castle and castle demesne ate in the great timbered hall. It seemed great to Emma then for she had seen nothing larger.

Emma followed her mother in order to go up the wooden steps to the solar, which was built against the end wall at one end of the hall and formed a cross gable. It was the time of day to begin her embroidery.

Engret approached the Lady Isolda. Engret had quarters over the gatehouse and was in a position of trust.

They moved out of earshot across the hall as Emma went on up the steps to the solar.

She had picked up her embroidery and had set a few stitches when Geva, her mother's maid came in.

'Lady Emma, your mother has sent me to take you back to speak to her.'

Once more standing in the hall Emma looked questioningly at her mother.

The Lady Isolda appeared thoughtful.

'Daughter,' she smiled faintly. 'You are to go with Geva to the dog court. Wandril the huntsman will give you the latest report on your father's favourite hound, Ascur. Listen carefully to what he has to say for I wish to send news of him back to your father tomorrow.'

Emma's face lit up. 'You have heard from my father?'

'Good news,' replied her mother, 'He is in good health and hopes to be home in September. Oh! And before I forget — the chapman has arrived. I will see him later with his wares. You may look at his trinkets on your way back from the dog court.'

Emma almost skipped beside Geva on her way to the kennel.

It was thirty feet long and fifteen feet wide, raised above the ground on timber stilts.

The grass on which it was built was in the sun all day. One of the two doors was always open in the daytime so that the hounds could go out at will. They could not go too far however as the dog court was surrounded by a palisade.

Leofric, the dog boy, slept in the kennel to keep the hounds from fighting.

When Emma opened the slatted gate in the fence she could see ten year old Leofric. He was sitting on a small upturned barrel spinning horse hair to make couples for the hounds.

He greeted Emma respectfully but there was a twinkle in his eye. He knew that she should have been sitting at her embroidery.

Wandril came from behind the kennel, carrying a lead of leather, well tawed.

Emma gave him her mother's message. He went to fetch Ascur, who was tethered by himself.

Wandril held Ascur on the end of the leather lead, and walked him up and down for Emma to inspect him.

She would not have known the hound's leg to have been broken, so well had it healed.

Wandril had put four splints on the leg, and bound them with flax wetted in white of egg, until the bones had knitted well together.

Emma stood talking to Wandril and Leofric for a short time, giving the good news about her father, then asking each about his family.

Wandril's wife had been the dairy maid. Leofric's father was the hayward; his older brother the cowherd who blew his horn in the trackway at the centre of the tofts each morning at dawn.

When the villagers heard it they started off their cows towards the cowherd, and he drove them to the common land to graze all day.

Emma then returned to the dog court gate on her way back to the bailey.

The sun was in Emma's eyes as Geva opened the gate. Emma put up her hand to shade her eyes as she turned towards the bailey with Geva, who closed the gate carefully.

The travelling chapman was unpacking his wares and spreading them out on a horse blanket in front of the bakehouse wall, watched by as many of the Manor's children as could escape from their tasks.

Emma abandoned dignity, joined the group and sat on a mounting block to watch, with her back to the brewhouse.

There were girdles, pins, needles, embroidered linen kerchiefs, brooches, buckles, mirrors, bandeaus, ribbons, combs, belts.

Emma had first handling of everything — but had no silver with which to buy.

Her mother would purchase anything she considered desirable for her daughter's use.

But this was only part of the thrill of the chapman's visit.

The children settled comfortably to hear the chapman's latest tale. They preferred tales of gallantry — but today it was of love.

Made spine chillingly scandalous by the chapman's voice. A tale he had collected in Northamptonshire concerning one Berengar le Moyne — nineteen, young, fatherless, good looking — but still under the guardianship of William of York, Provost of Beverley, a strict churchman.

The chapman went on with his story, in a voice that carried to his audience.

'This Berengar, last year, fell under the seductive spell of a woman in his future Manor of Bernewelle, which he visited when allowed leave from his squire's duties. His mother Roysia still lived in the castle and guarded his interests. Well, on one of his visits home he had come across the luscious Diote, a bondwoman and young widow of his late father's miller.'

The chapman looked round the semi-circle of youngsters.

'What do you think happened next?'

There was a sigh of anticipation from his audience.

'Yes, soon the ravishing Diote was occupying quarters at a discreet homestead in the forest, with young Lord Berengar a besotted visitor.'

The audience gasped with appreciation.

'There was someone young Berengar had forgotten however.'

'The Provost of Beverley,' breathed the chapman's audience.

'Yes, the Provost of Beverley, William of York himself. He now took a guiding hand. Young Berengar was sent back to his military training, after which service he was to be knighted. He left Diote well provided for until his return from the war in Wales.'

A whisper of relief went round the watching faces.

'Provost William provided an even better portion for Diote. The silver was found for the price of her manumission at the Manor Court. She was married quite joyfully to a very willing and well paid freeman from one of the Beverley Manors — with commendable speed, and before Berengar returned from Wales that year. Being just nineteen he naturally uttered vows of celibacy, repudiated womenkind, and hurried back to the Welsh wars.'

Emma's childish thoughts turned to her father — fighting there. She wondered idly if he had ever met this young man Berengar le Moyne.

The chapman was now finishing his story with a denunciation of young Lord Berengar's deflowering of an innocent maiden.

Emma interrupted.

'Not so,' — breaking through the general assent.

'The woman was not a maiden. She encouraged him to think she was in love with him. She only wished for his silver. He will get over it.'

The chapman turned quickly towards Emma.

Then his eyes widened, his mouth opened; no words came out; he gulped convulsively and seemed to be gazing with a thunderstruck expression at a point behind Emma.

Emma turned towards the open brewhouse door behind her — but could see nothing to account for the chapman's expression.

Nothing moved; the wall was a blank.

The chapman muttered and began quickly to gather his trinkets together.

Hanfrid came over from the main door to escort the chapman to the Lady Isolda — and the group dispersed.

Emma had heard no more of the story of the tale's hero (or villain) until that morning, when she had so badly needed a hero to appear.

10

Glancing sideways Emma studied the hero.

Warworn, lean of cheek, tough, sitting straight in the saddle, and now four experienced years older.

Now also nearing the Trent river on his way south with his new bride.

Emma wondered thoughtfully if he had kept his vow of celibacy when the fair Diote had abandoned him.

Or had he thought better of his vow and found consolation in the arms of a succession of beautiful Diotes?

A question Emma could hardly ask him.

Soon she could see a low line of hills.

'The Trent river flows this side of the hills,' — curtly from her husband.

A man was walking towards them from the direction of the river. He walked with the aid of a staff, for the weight on his back was bending him over.

The woven willow wand creel stretched cone shaped from his thighs to his head. It was full of eels, alive and wriggling.

They reached the Trent at Gunthorpe. There was a ferry — for which Emma was quite thankful. The river was the largest and deepest she had ever seen.

Sir Berengar summoned the ferryman to row Emma across the river. She climbed into the rowing boat, holding up her gown and cloak carefully, and sat down on the stern seat indicated by her husband.

Sir Berengar told the ferryman to wait until he had taken his men and horses across the ford before starting to row.

The current rocked the boat gently as they waited.

'Waleran — you wait behind here until the Lady Emma reaches the opposite bank of the river,' commanded her husband.

Waleran was the senior of the three Bernewelle men, grizzled of hair, and trustworthy.

Emma watched as the horses waded across the ford. (Her horse was led.) The water rose to their knees, then higher, until they were nigh to swimming at the far, deeper side, where they had to scramble up the shingle.

Sir Berengar waved to the boatman to set off.

Not until Emma had been helped from the boat and on to the far river bank was Waleran signalled to set off across the ford.

He had kicked his feet free of the stirrups

before entering the river.

Just as his horse found a grip on the shingle of the far side, to leave the water, he stumbled badly, throwing Waleran into the river.

Emma ran towards the water's edge, being nearest, only to hear a lashing voice ordering her back.

She took no notice; continued towards the river bank, was pinioned helplessly by merciless hands, deposited on the ground; and rolled round in time to see Sir Berengar hauling a sodden, dripping Waleran on to the shingle.

Waleran received a tirade and was despatched into the bushes to change into dry clothes from the pack horse's saddle bag. His own horse had followed him out of the water.

Emma remained in a sitting position, arms round knees, with her chin resting on her knees, looking what she hoped, was suitably disgusted.

Her husband's hand grasped her wrist, jerked her to her feet and led her some way away from his men, beside an oak, whence he delivered a blistering reproof.

'Never again interfere with the men's welfare. However perilous a situation arises, you, my lady, are not to intervene. You are also to obey my orders at once, and without question.'

Emma's chin went up. She did not actually say the word 'No,' but she looked full into her husband's face and gazed the defiance.

His eyes narrowed.

He took a quick step towards her, grasped her shoulders and gave her a quick shake.

'My girl, I make you a promise — if you disobey me I swear I will beat you soundly, if it has to be in front of my men or any other who is present. For the moment, it is finished. Come, we must eat.'

He led Emma to a grassy bank where the food was being laid out for their meal.

Still simmering, Emma sat on the grassy bank beside Sir Berengar, turning a haughty shoulder as she ate the bread and meat, and pretended to be interested in the swallows skimming the water.

Sir Berengar munched abstractedly, picking up a stick and drawing pictures with it on a patch of sand at his feet.

Emma got up and stepped away to behind the bankside.

Waleran came over from the group of men to speak to Sir Berengar.

He stood gazing at the pictures, pointed, and asked a question.

'Bernewelle le Moyne, as I plan it to be,' replied his master.

Emma pricked up her ears — and wished she had not turned her back on the proceedings.

He continued, 'I shall build a little way south east, away from the present motte — some twenty feet above the Bernewelle Brook, and up the side valley opening on to the main valley of the Nene River.'

Emma saw Waleran point to a place in the picture and look a question.

'Enfilading of the wall?'

'See — round towers projecting at the angles of the wall to prevent that. I plan to build the castle of Bernewelle of limestone — walls thirty feet high, twelve feet thick, with battlements. The gatehouse will have a portcullis — here.' He pointed.

The discussion ranged on, until Waleran returned with his orders to the group of men.

Emma had twisted the meadow flowers into a circlet by now.

Curiosity drove her back to the grassy knoll and the pictures in the sand. She subsided gracefully, with assumed carelessness, and glanced at the drawings in the sand.

Then, puzzled, she looked up at Sir Berengar.

His eyes were shining with enthusiasm.

'Of stone,' he said simply.

'Tell me,' Emma pointed to the second picture — for the first picture was plain to see — a castle, with walls and round towers and a gatehouse, drawn in the sand.

But the second picture Emma could not interpret.

He picked up the stick and traced round the edges of the plan.

'Pretend you are a kestrel high in the air. Look down from straight above my castle — and that is the shape you will see.'

'A castle of stone,' he emphasised again — then a quickly veiled glance, 'Now I have your dower lands.'

'So I represent the future stones,' — bitterly from Emma.

He dropped the stick; the glow faded.

He held out a hand, stern again, unsmiling, 'Come, we lose time.'

Emma bit back the quick apology that rose to her lips. Better this way. Let him think her indifferent — nay — boorish. Emma did not desire his overture of friendliness — or was she only trying to convince herself.

Once again in the saddle she looked at the sky. Clouds were gathering in front of the sun.

Soon they reached a wider track that ran,

very straight, south west.

'The Roman Fosse Way,' laconically from her husband. 'We do not follow it for long. It is too frequented for our journey.'

Emma knew that he thought of Gerold and the threat of ambush.

At a junction of ways they turned left, off the main track to Leicester, towards Broughton.

The sun had now been obscured by cloud completely, mist was rising from the valley and though it was summer Emma began to feel cold and desolate.

Even the light was now fading; shadows were lengthening. For some time her husband had been looking right and left of the track, missing nothing.

Suddenly he gave an order, grasped Emma's rein and led them from the track — turning right towards a wood on the valley side.

Flanking the trees by the wood's edge was a dilapidated barn, being used now more as an open cart shelter than a barn. But once through the door there was enough timbering left without gaps, to hide the group from other travellers on the road.

The horses were hidden at one end of the building. Straw was pulled from the heap in the corner to form rough pallets for the men's comfort — three piles a foot apart for the men. Two farther along, behind a cart for Emma and her husband.

Sir Berengar detailed the order of the watch throughout the night, appointing a man in turn, on duty.

Emma lay down on the straw heap designated as hers and wrapped her cloak round her. She felt cold, damp, dreary and hopeless.

The mutter of mens' voices died down as they stretched out at the other end of the barn on their pallets of straw.

Emma began to think of her father; to picture him eating his lonely meal; to see the sconces of the castle going out one by one, until all was moonlight, as it was here in the cart shed.

Emma pictured her father crying out in the night, asking for water to drink, nobody hearing, and his enfeebled hands clutching at the covers, trying to raise himself.

Her husband stirred and stretched out on his pallet, a foot away from hers — and was still. Now surely he slept.

Emma buried her face against her arm to stifle the sobs. Her mind searched for courage, yet faltered. She wished desperately for the oblivion of sleep.

She was still sobbing almost silently when

she was jerked unceremoniously across the gap between the straw heaps, and clamped against her husband's side, with her head forced against his shoulder, his left arm round under her breast, holding her back against him, and his right hand gripping her wrists.

He let her struggle until her breath gave out and she lay quiet but rigid against him.

'Stop grieving,' his voice whispered, 'Your father has given you a chance — take it.'

Emma's face was turned away, rejecting his pity.

Then, lying stiffly against his side, suddenly she gasped, affronted anew. He was blowing gently down her ear.

She disdained to notice — moving her head another inch away — then smothered a yelp as he bit the ear with a noticeable nip.

Emma jerked round, incensed, to look up at him in the dimness.

The grey eyes were understanding.

'You keep me awake, Kyndel,' he said gently.

Emma was desperately trying to read his face. The impression that his intentions were of a far more active nature than slumber began to fade.

He grinned appreciatively at her expression of relief.

'Curl up and go to sleep,' — a gently chiding murmur.

'You hurt my wrists.'

'Do I?' He laughed softly and shifted his grip.

The warmth of his body was creeping through to Emma. Her head slid back into the hollow of his shoulder.

From the armpit seeped the acrid smell of damp, sweaty, wool and leather, comfortingly familiar.

Emma tried to keep alert and tensed against him but the insidious feeling of warmth and comfort and safety closed her eyelids.

She sighed, nuzzled against his shoulder, and contrary to all reason, slept.

She woke, alone, to find her husband's cloak tucked round her.

11

They regained the trackway just before dawn, and continued on their way to Melton Mowbray, where a bridge crossed the River Eye. The townspeople looked at them with no more than the usual interest accorded to travellers.

Sir Berengar's men wore no badge. His coat of arms had been removed from the tunics of his men before ever setting forth from Bernewelle le Moyne. They were just another group of travellers, somewhat dusty.

Once clear of the last toft of Melton Mowbray Sir Berengar gave a terse order to his men. They awaited his further instructions — so perforce did Emma.

He spoke grimly. 'Three miles ahead lies Burton Lazars, the chief Lazar House in the country. You are permitted to give alms to any leper you see if you so desire — but no one of you — (he looked at Emma sternly) will ride closer to a leper than twelve feet. You will throw down the alms and if you speak at all you will stay your distance on the windward side.'

He wheeled his horse and forward they went.

In the distance Emma could see a figure with his back to them — limping along by the side of the road. He was clothed in a black habit.

As they drew nearer, in single file, well to the opposite side of the track, Emma could see that the man's feet were swathed in ragged bandages, and were covered by roughly made boots. He carried the leper's rattle in one hand and shook it vigorously as they approached.

It was of wood, with a handle grip. Made in one piece with the handle was the central rigid clapper. The two side clappers were hinged to the base of the centre one and had a piece of leather holding the three parts together, and leaving enough space for the clappers to move a few inches when the handle was shaken.

Sir Berengar tossed a coin to the man, so accurately, that it fell in a way that he could easily have caught it — only when the free hand came out of the wide sleeve to catch the coin it missed — for the hand had no fingers or thumb.

There were just slight stumps where fingers should have been — each with a central dark core — like a bunch of carrots that has had the tops sliced off.

The leper picked up the coin with his good

left hand, having tucked the clapper under his right arm as they passed.

The group was now approaching the gateway to the Lazar House.

The buildings inside were of stone, surrounded by a dry moat, with a separate house for the master, and several fish ponds to supply the needs of the community.

Another desolate figure sat by the roadside a little way from the gate.

Emma probed her fingers into the soft leather of the draw string purse attached to her girdle and tossed her contribution to the leper, with a heartfelt prayer.

This leper had his black hood clutched about his face but Emma's throw had been somewhat high for him to reach and the coin hit the wall behind him. Trying to catch it he dropped his rattle, stretched up his arms, his head went back and his hood fell back also.

Emma shivered, gasped, and urged her horse to a faster pace — for the leper had no recognisable face — just a mass of excrescences, with two fleshy protuberances for eyes, a slit with thickenings above and below for a mouth, and no nose. It was the face of a fluffed up cat.

Sir Berengar caught Emma's bridle and rode beside her. The men crossed themselves as they cantered on. They all breathed more easily once beyond the boundary of Burton Lazars, across the Burton Brook and riding downhill.

'How many live there?' Emma asked.

'Twelve is usual,' her husband replied.

'Will they never go back to their families?'

'No, not if they have been segregated. Once a man is pronounced a leper it is the priest's duty to publish a decree in the parish church. The following Sunday the parish priest meets the leper (who now has to dress in black) at a place outside the town, takes him to the church and there in a place set apart administers the last mass. Afterwards the priest takes a handful of sand and pronounces the words, 'Henceforth be dead to the world and live in God.' Then he reads out the list of things prohibited to a leper — from walking barefoot to inheriting property.'

Emma crossed herself again; prayed again for the souls of the inmates of Burton Lazars and again gave heartfelt thanks that this scourge of leprosy had not yet touched close to her family.

Soon they splashed through another brook. She could see a cluster of buildings on the left — 'Whissendine' — from her husband. Another two miles and there was a church to the left of the road — 'Langham', laconically. 'We make good progress. See there is Oakham in front of us. As we pass through the village look to the left and you will see the Ferrars Hall of stone.'

Emma looked with interest and saw the largest building of stone she had ever beheld.

'It was said that de Ferrars had been farrier to the army of King William the Bastard.'

The next few miles were up hill and down dale until they were climbing the steeper slope to the church of Uppingham, built on a ridge.

Then on again, still riding south, past the track to Lyddington on the left and Stoke Dry on the right.

As they breasted the hill, and the track turned on the shoulder of it — there before them was spread an extensive rolling vista — the valley of the Welland, the winding river with its lush green water meadows on either side, and the escarpment beyond the river.

Emma had, without thinking, drawn rein to drink in the view of green meadows, green, green, and yet more luscious green. Her husband drew rein also; the others followed suit.

He looked amused, but pointed out the remaining landmarks.

'The River Welland flows from right to left. To the right, upstream, lies Harborough. To the left downstream lies Stamford, both quite out of sight. To the right the track descends, crosses the water meadows, goes over a timbered bridge and up the hillside. Halfway up the hill is the massive stone pile of Rockingham Castle.'

He pointed — 'There is the rounded keep, the curtain walls enclosing the inner and outer bailey. Within is a large stone hall.'

There was a bare, steep, slope from the keep and main gateway down to the track, and a bare, steep, slope down towards the river.

'The Welland River is the boundary between north and south. In the old days, to the north was under the jurisdiction and settlement of the Danes. Land is still measured there in caracutes, while to the south it is measured in hides.'

They descended gradually to a hamlet at the level of the water meadows.

Emma looked a question. 'Caldecott,' he replied — 'From here to Rockingham is flat — the Welland's flood plain.'

He was frowning, looking anxiously at the sky. Following his glance Emma could see dark, threatening clouds above the ridge in front, clouds that were a leaden colour, with a pale streak at their flurried edges.

'Storm,' Sir Berengar murmured.

Emma saw a streak of lightning strike through the leaden mass, and heard the faint sound of far off thunder.

Her husband swore beneath his breath.

'The high land between the Welland and the Nene attracts storms. Come — we must cross the river before it rises.'

The horses were urged into a canter across the flat, green plain.

There was more lightning now, though it was still over the ridge.

Raindrops began to fall; a rain haze was over the ridge, blotting out the castle in a steady downpour.

The river was already rising, flowing brown and angry beneath the timber bridge whose main supports were of oak trunks across the river.

They dismounted and led the horses. Waleran, Sir Berengar's sergeant led Emma's mount as well as his own.

Emma's husband gripped her wrist firmly and did not release her until they were on the other side of the bridge — away from the whirling eddies of frothy, foam flecked water, away from the flotsam and jetsam carried down willy nilly by the angry flood.

'That way.' Sir Berengar pointed to a track

that ran south west, almost parallel to the river bank, upstream, but on higher land than the river.

'The direct route is straight up Rockingham Hill and through Corby village. We cannot take that way now. It is better to avoid the risk of ambush and take a different route.'

The rain was soaking through Emma's cloak to the fur lining. It came almost straight down in an unending downpour. The splashes spluttered up with some force as they hit the ground.

The lightning seemed all around them, as flash followed flash, and the thunder reverberated along the hillside.

Emma realised that, bedraggled and streaming water, they were skirting Rockingham Castle demesne and were about to ascend the ridge at a point two miles upstream from Rockingham.

'Cottingham,' breathed her lord, 'Here we turn and follow the old Roman Road.'

By now they were all soaked, almost to the skin and Emma was beginning to shiver uncontrollably.

The ground rose steeply. They toiled past a cluster of tofts at the crossroads. Emma wondered why Sir Berengar did not ask for shelter here.

Sheep were huddled under a moveable

straw thatched fold near the track but the rest of the close cropped dell was blotted out by rain.

By the time the group reached the top of the hill the thunder was lessening and the rain was but a thin drizzle. As they came to the crossroads along the top of the ridge even the drizzle had stopped.

A sudden shaft of sunlight lit the writhing arms of the oak beside them. Its canopy of leaves was transformed at once into a shimmering expanse of trembling green. Every curlicued leaf became intensely alive.

Every blade of grass beneath the tree stood out, spear like, silhouetted, with its droplet of water sparkling back the light.

Sir Berengar was frowning.

'We must dry out, and eat.'

He consulted with Waleran — 'We go to Knight's Lodge — the hall house of a long term friend of my family. There we shall find shelter, food and warmth.'

The group was following a track that ran south again.

Oak forest was on either side of the track.

'Pipewell Abbey is two miles beyond the trees.' He pointed to the right.

12

On the left the line of trees ceased. There extended beside the track a forest 'lawn', an extensive clearance of the trees for fields within the forest area.

The buildings were in two separate areas, each roughly rectangular, lying alongside the main track and separated from each other by a side track at right angles to the main trackway.

First the weary group passed farm buildings, within a palisade of upright, pointed timbers forming a rectangle beside the track.

On the nearside was an open cart shed with two carts lying idle under its roof. On the far side was a well kept barn, flanked by barns on either side of that, completing the rectangle of buildings, with two stables.

The whole formed a separate enclosure from the hall-house, which was built also within a rectangularly laid out plot, surrounded by a moat twelve feet wide, beside the main track.

The company turned down the minor track and reached the entrance bridge of wooden planks that straddled the moat, up to the strong gate in another palisade. This palisade was built all around the edge of the moat on the inner side and enclosed all the homestead buildings.

Standing, awaiting the group's arrival, which had been heralded by clucking hens, quacking ducks and barking dogs (not to mention the interested gaze of a cowman bringing his small herd along the farm track from the field beyond) was the benevolent owner of the 'Lawn' — Sir Henry de Braiboc.

Sir Henry held out his hands to Sir Berengar and greeted him as a son.

'Welcome, welcome, Berengar le Moyne, to my poor house. God's bones, but you are the image of your father. Of age now, aren't you? Heaven be praised. Not that I have ought against a churchman — but William of York is a stern man for a guardian. And who is this?' turning to Emma.

'May I present you to my wife, the Lady Emma,' replied Sir Berengar.

'My dear child,' said Sir Henry, 'Come in at once, you are soaked — both of you.'

He ushered them into a hall of modest proportions, with a fire of logs blazing in the centre.

Orders to his servants to look after the three le Moyne men were soon given. The horses were led across to the stables to be rubbed down, fed, and watered.

He gave up the solar for the use of Emma and Sir Berengar.

A wench, Gundrea, from the pantry, conducted Emma up the wooden steps at the gable end of the hall, and into the solar.

Gundrea helped Emma to strip off her wet garments, towelled her dry, and wrapped a blanket round her.

Emma's husband did not follow them. He stayed with his men by the hall fire, their saddle bags were brought in and they quickly stripped, towelled, and changed into dry clothes.

Emma's saddle bag was dumped outside the solar door for the girl Gundrea to bring into the small room. Emma quickly dressed in a dry shift, underdress and gown. Her dripping cloak and other garments were taken away to be dried. She wore the red gown embroidered round the neck slit with turquoise blue.

By the time Emma reappeared down the steps to the hall the small troop had vanished to their duties. Only her husband remained with Sir Henry de Braiboc. Sir Henry put Emma at her ease straight away.

'My felicitations, Sir Berengar, you rogue.

You have made an excellent choice of a bride. I wish my son and his wife were here with me to welcome her. Unfortunately Sir Wischard is occupied with a legal claim in Northampton and has taken his lady with him, to visit her parents near there until the business is finished. My grandson is here, however, at the Lodge.'

He smiled proudly. 'A young man of fifteen years, and six feet tall already! You will meet him when we break bread. In the meantime I propose to take you both on a tour of the property.'

The hall-house was of brownish grey stone with grey stone tiles for a roof, already splattered with rusty hued lichen.

The hall was almost in the centre of the moated rectangle and was built parallel to the main track by which they had approached, from north to south.

Across the near end, at right angles to the hall and joined to it was a two storied gable end — built to the height of the hall — with the small solar above, and the pantry-buttery below.

There was a separate timber kitchen beyond the hall, nearer to the far section of the moat, leaving sufficient distance between the two buildings to avoid a risk of a fire spreading from the kitchen to the hall-house.

The prevailing wind blew from north to south so that the sparks from the kitchen fires would be carried away from the hall-house.

Sir Henry led Sir Berengar and Emma outside of the house and pointed out the single plank that led from behind the house, across the moat, to two dog kennels, also palisaded.

The hounds were allowed to roam free within the moated area during the night.

Emma noticed a strange rounded object embedded in the clayey earth at the edge of the moat's bank, and stooped to pick it up.

She rinsed the sticky earth from it in the water of the moat. She held something that was about an inch and a half long, greyish and striated.

It looked like a snail shell — but it was turned to stone — even the inside of the shell was not empty but was grey stone.

Sir Henry glanced at it, in the palm of Emma's hand. 'A Giant's toenail, the villagers call it. There are many such in the fields around here.'

Emma put it in her draw string purse, for a talisman.

By the time they returned to the hall the trestle tables were being put up: the one at the solar end of the hall for the master's family and guests, the two flanking tables down the length of the hall for everyone else.

The trenchers were being put in place as were the benches also.

Emma went into the hall-house, leaving Sir Berengar to saunter over the drawbridge, across the minor track, towards the farm buildings.

Emma went up to the solar to put away the grey snail stone safely in her saddle bag.

She strolled idly over to the small window that looked out across the moat and drawbridge to the enclosure of farm buildings.

Emma watched Gundrea (who she had last seen fetching bread from the pantry) walk over the drawbridge, then slip furtively into the barn.

She did not reappear. But Sir Berengar did. Nonchalantly progressing from inspecting the horses in the stable, to striding across the centre space, and stepping quickly through the doorway of the barn.

Emma's hands clenched. She resolutely made herself count the timbers in the drawbridge.

She counted eight, and counted eight again, and again, and again, and went on counting until tears of mortification ran down her cheeks.

Why did it matter so much?

Why should it hurt her that this near stranger should fancy a little light diversion in swiving a serving maid?

Emma's hands gripped together. She leaned her head against the cold stone of the window embrasure, and looked out through a haze of tears.

True, Sir Berengar had been somewhat kind to her, in the cart shed, last night. Mayhap he would have been similarly kind to a damp and lonely hound lost during the hunt. It meant nothing.

'Face it fool,' she thought, 'You hoped he would love you in time. So — he married you only for your dower lands — you will have to accept the degree of wifehood he ordains for you — and it does not include tantrums about his extra-marital wenches.'

Her lord appeared at length, whistling happily as he sauntered back to the moat and crossed the drawbridge towards the hall.

Emma turned away from the window, splashed cold water from the pitcher on to her face, dried it slowly, then sat on the wooden chest by the bed and let cold, furious anger take over.

By the time Gundrea tapped on the solar

door Emma was ready, and went down to break bread with her chin up, her eyes glittering and a determination to show her lord that what was sauce for the gander was sauce for the goose also.

Sir Henry's grandson Tancred awaited her by the high table.

His eyes widened and a look of frank admiration swept over his face as his grandfather presented him to Emma.

Emma smiled at him with what she hoped was a bewitching smile, fluttered her eyelashes and murmured in an awed tone, 'Why, how tall you are!'

Tancred visibly grew another inch.

Sir Berengar gave his wife a quick, surprised glance and thereafter preserved a calm and unruffled front.

Emma had Tancred sitting at her right hand side. She chatted gaily to him throughout the meal and laughed merrily at his anecdotes, whether of hunting or hawking.

When Tancred used a platter to represent a castle which was to be stormed by his imaginary troops, Emma let her sleeve brush against his hand as she pointed to the supposed moat.

All this Sir Berengar observed without a blink.

Tancred looked down at the vivid young

face on a level with his shoulder; at the dark curling hair escaping from under the fine linen veil, the slim deliciously curved figure, the long delicate fingers toying with her goblet of wine — and was lost.

He had been a page and a squire in a large household but had never been so close to so enchanting a creature.

Sir Berengar, in between his conversations with Sir Henry, thought morosely, 'My God, she does not even know how powerful her charm is. The unfortunate youth has no need of a bucketful at a time. Now, how to resolve this without affront. And how to discover the cause of it.'

Tancred responded ever more freely as the level of his wine cup became lower.

By the time the meal was over he was gazing into Emma's eyes worshipfully and trying to hold her hand under the tablecloth.

His grandfather had several times glanced at Sir Berengar but Sir Berengar's voice did not alter. He maintained a flow of inconsequential conversation with his host.

Emma was in the middle of a peal of flatteringly amused laughter at a riposte of Tancred's when a serving boy hovered to refill her wine cup.

She turned and gestured the boy to fill it and so looked full into Sir Berengar's grim, forbidding countenance.

His hand quietly covered her cup.

The serving boy melted away unbidden.

Emma's chin went up — 'My Lord?' she began — and got no further.

Her husband rose, tight lipped, took her wrist in an iron clasp, bowed to his host and ground out with freezing formality, 'Lady, I escort you to your chamber.'

Emma looked up at him questioningly — and went.

He looked stern enough to be quite capable of carrying her ignominiously from the board.

He handed her up the steps and through the doorway of the solar. He closed the door on her in silence and went back to his host, leaving Emma shaking a little but unrepentant.

Much later Emma stood attired in her long, white, pleated shift, by the window embrasure, sliding the dark plaits of hair loose with fingers that trembled, and with her back to the door.

Footsteps sounded outside, strong, heavy, purposeful footsteps.

Sir Berengar came in, closed the door dispiritedly and trod wearily to the chest.

Emma stole a look over her shoulder. He was frowning, thoughtful.

His leather purse thudded to the top of the chest; the leather belt and sheathed dagger followed it.

Emma turned, swallowed, and forced the waver out of her voice.

'I suppose you are going to beat me,' — knowing her behaviour well merited a husbandly beating.

'No,' he said, in an oddly flat tone. 'No, I'm not going to beat you,' stretching his arms, stripping off his tunic, then his shirt.

The colour rose over Emma's face. He was naked to the waist.

The candlelight flickered over the white skin of well-muscled shoulders. He wore braies of fine linen, folded over the waist string. The crossed linen folds ended at the knee leaving a corner of the white triangular material loose.

Each hose ended mid thigh in two points to which a string was attached. This looped over the braies waist string and tied the hose back and front.

The swathe of linen over the thighs emphasised the length of limb beneath.

Sir Berengar's eyes were narrowed and unsmiling, and his mouth was grim.

Emma's glance met his and she read his purpose.

'No,' she breathed.

He studied the shirt still in his hands as though he'd never seen it before.

'You leave me no other choice. Come, let there be an end. Tonight you become my wife — maybe then you will learn to behave as a wife should.'

He stood with the moonlight striking his powerful arms and shoulders, his chest strangely white against the brown of his face.

'No, and no, and no,' said Emma bitterly, seeing again the vision of the wench Gundrea going into the barn.

'No?' His eyebrows went up. In two strides he had Emma's hands pinned behind her. 'No?'

He was breathing fast. She felt his arms tighten, and as his head came down Emma twisted wildly and bit as hard as she could into the corded muscle at the top of his naked arm.

His breath hissed in. One hand grasped a handful of Emma's dark hair, and jerked her head back. His mouth closed down savagely on hers, blotting out moonlight, candlelight, into velvet blackness.

Emma was shaking when he loosened his grip.

Tears slid down her face and on to his shoulder.

The touch of his naked skin was exquisite purgatory.

'Mother of God, why her?'

Emma did not realise she had spoken aloud.

Sir Berengar shook her. 'Why who?'

'The wench you took to lie with in the barn.'

He studied her face.

'So that is it.'

He let her go suddenly, and smiled, his mouth curving up in a laugh of amused relief.

Emma leaned back with her cheek against the cool stone of the window embrasure and gasped.

Her husband did not look in the least perturbed.

He cast her a measuring glance then threw himself on the bed with his hands locked behind his head.

The red marks of the bite stood out against the white of his arm — two rows of beautifully even teeth marks.

Emma's throat went dry.

'You saw — what?'

'I saw the wench go into the barn. I saw you follow . . . and . . . ' her voice wavered, 'It was a long time before you came out.'

He whistled between his teeth.

'So you thought me frolicking in the hay?'

Emma bit her lip.

'You did not see Waleran go in before the girl?'

'No.'

'Kyndel, she is his daughter. She had news for us of traveller's tales. We hoped to hear of Sir Gerold's movements. We must needs go singly and carefully to speak with her. A cousin of Sir Gerold's sergeant is a groom here.'

He explained as though speaking to a child.

'Dear God,' Emma thought, 'What comes to me now?'

So much for her suspicions. She could not look at him. Her fingers twisted a strand of hair round and round until it curled in an ebony ring round her finger.

'Well?' he said.

'I'm sorry,' Emma whispered and hid her face in her hands.

He swung off the bed and came to her, leaning his back against the angled wall of the embrasure and putting out his left arm to cut off her escape.

Emma faced him.

'Now, my lady, you owe me reparation.'

He glanced at the mark on his arm and

his eyes gleamed — 'This shall be your first lesson in the married state.'

Her husband drew her gently towards him, still leaning his shoulders against the stone wall, and held her tightly within the circle of his arms until she touched his chest.

It was strange to be so close and Emma swallowed nervously.

She sensed his eyes glinting as his head came down. His lips brushed her eyelids gently, one after the other, travelled across her forehead and down.

His hand gentled her face, touching her cheek and stroking her hair back.

His lips followed, then travelled on fleetingly to her mouth.

Emma gasped and trembled as his lips nuzzled from side to side, then pressed down firmly but so lightly on her mouth.

She felt her hands slide round his shoulders and her lips fluttered in response.

His head came up and he laughed, holding Emma still against his shoulder.

'This for the first lesson,' he kissed her again quickly.

A gentle push — 'Get you to bed lady, between the sheets. I lie on the covers, with the spare one over me — saving my word to your father.'

He fell asleep quickly with the practised

ease of the campaigner.

Emma lay in the flickering shadows pondering on the inexplicable ways of men — her husband in particular.

Tonight her husband had ended by showing her forbearance and tenderness, for which she was duly grateful — but a small portion of her mind remained regretful, regretful that he had been quite so forbearing.

13

Next morning the small troop followed the main track towards the King's Wood. Just as they had approached a cross track the pace of Turold's horse altered.

The off hind shoe had become loose.

Sir Berengar shrugged with resignation. 'The smithy at Corby — we must then take the Oundle road through Weldon: a pity — for it is a treacherous track.'

After turning towards Corby the trees seemed to grow more densely.

Sometimes the sun struck through a gap in the canopy of leaves, lighting the shining white bark of a birch, darkly pock marked.

The trees were mostly oak, with twisted branches, and bark seamed with brown furrows.

The ground beneath the horses' hoofs had that springy resilience of a woodland path.

The trees began to thin and there ahead lay the grey church and a cluster of tofts — Corby — where they would find the farrier.

Soon the troop dismounted for the welcome break.

As Emma's husband swung her from the

saddle his strong arms held her for a moment longer than was strictly necessary. He looked down at her quizzically until colour flooded from her neck over her face.

Sir Berengar found an upturned keg for Emma to sit on while the horse was shod.

The brazier was glowing red. The farrier and his assistant each wore a leather apron divided just above the knee, to splay out and cover each leg.

The anvil shone silver, polished with use. Near it was a wooden skip of tools.

When the horse shoe had been replaced the group remounted and turned down the track to Weldon, a village in the forest where several tracks met.

'At night a light always burns in the church tower,' observed Sir Berengar, 'To serve as a beacon for anyone lost in the forest.'

Sir Berengar pointed out that he intended to take the Oundle track, which involved riding through and just beyond the village, then making a sharp, double bend turn to the right.

The way was so narrow, one side being against a toft wall that the company had to ride in single file.

Sir Berengar led the file. Emma was next to the last, saving only Waleran, who had orders to protect her in an emergency.

Suddenly there was a shout from Sir Berengar, 'Back Waleran,' and the clash of arms.

Waleran forced his horse close against the wall, dragged Emma's rein round and bade her ride fast back on her tracks and turn left at the fork in the village — he would overtake her.

He did, cantering recklessly — but holding the rein of Sir Berengar's horse, with her husband bent over the horse's neck, clinging to his mane.

'Ride,' gasped Waleran, 'Turold and Segar are delaying them. They are Sir Gerold's men. If we can gain a little I can draw them off. I know this country hood blind.'

They had almost left the Weldon quarry land behind when Waleran pointed, 'When we are level with that oak — a solitary tree — draw rein quickly and dismount.'

Emma obeyed and slid rapidly from the saddle.

Waleran hauled her husband from his saddle, supported his weight and stumbled towards the dense bushes beside the oak.

Sir Berengar's arm was across Waleran's shoulder as he staggered behind the bushes. As Waleran relinquished his hold Sir Berengar subsided on to the ground.

'Lie out of sight beside Sir Berengar,'

Waleran panted. 'When the pursuit has gone by line up the oak with the hawthorn at the opposite side of the field. Then walk towards the hawthorn. There is an abandoned 'fox-hole' mine — as there are still in use at Collyweston — in the centre of the field. Sir Gerold will not know of it. Hide there until dusk and I will return for you.'

Emma lay prone behind the bushes beside the battered figure of her husband, heard Waleran lead the horses back, then ride over their tracks with his horse and the two led horses. Their hoofbeats gradually grew fainter.

Not five minutes later more hoofbeats pounded. It sounded like a group of at least six men and horses.

Emma only hoped that Waleran did know the country hood blind.

She waited for ten more minutes then scrambled to her feet, lined up the oak with the hawthorn as instructed, shook Sir Berengar into half consciousness and dragged him to his feet.

He leaned on her heavily and she began to make her way, reeling under his weight, across the grassy field.

Suddenly the ground began to descend into a decline — about the width of a cart track, but grassed over like the rest of the ground.

It sloped gradually down towards the base of a grassy precipice.

Almost at the limit of Emma's endurance they lurched on until they reached below the level of normal ground, where they subsided, panting.

Fear drove Emma on but even after the short rest Sir Berengar could not stand, tug as she might.

She began to drag him along. He hauled himself where he could towards the entrance to the mine, beneath the precipice.

Blood still oozed from a gash across his temple.

By dint of resting between spasms of dragging his dead weight Emma reached the cave like entrance to the mine, gave a final pull and they were, at last, completely hidden from a casual glance down towards the sloping path.

Emma rested a little, sitting on the sandy floor of the mine.

The air was fresh and cool, though not cold, and certainly not damp as Emma had expected.

She sat breathing deeply and letting the fine pale silver sand from the floor of the mine trickle through her fingers.

The mine shaft branched just inside the entrance.

Emma took the right hand fork and heaved her burden along in the sand; pulling him strenuously until a bend in the cave shaft hid the light and the entrance from view.

Emma went back to the entrance and brushed her gown across the surface of the sand to cover their tracks.

Then she sat with her back against the rock of the shaft wall, and lifted her husband by the shoulders until his head rested on her lap.

In the darkness her fingers felt carefully over his hair until they reached the source of the sticky blood, oozing sluggishly.

Emma quickly reached to the back of her neck, untied the bow to the gown's back thongs — loosened them enough to pull down the gown over her shoulders and wriggle her arms out. She untied the neck string of the sleeveless undergown and pulled that down.

Then she tore round the armhole of the pleated sleeve of her shift until the whole sleeve tore away and she was equipped with enough material to form a bandage.

A piece ripped from one end was quickly fashioned into a makeshift pad and placed on the gash. The rest of the sleeve Emma tore into two strips, knotted them together to form a bandage and tied the pad in place.

Once her patient lay bandaged, but still conscious, Emma eased her cloak round gently so that it covered her husband and one of her shoulders.

He was still breathing deeply.

Emma began to pray, murmuring her petitions in a whisper.

Long after the last prayer had fallen into the black silence she sat listening for a foot fall at the entrance to the shaft.

Emma felt carefully round her husband's belt for his sheathed dagger.

The dagger was still in the sheath.

'Thanks be to Mary, Mother of God,' she murmured.

The silence loomed over Emma again.

There was a faint stir from Sir Berengar.

He groaned and moved his head slightly. His hands slid up to explore the bandage round his head. He swore faintly.

The hands travelled farther — to Emma's waist, up to slide over her breast and touch her hair.

'My Lord,' she faltered, 'You must lie still. The bandage is but a makeshift. If you dislodge it your wound may begin to bleed again.'

'Where the devil are we?' He sounded testy but still very weak.

'Hidden in a mine shaft — Waleran bade me hide with you until he could return in the dark with the horses. He took both our horses to decoy Gerold's men. He seemed quite confident that he could lead them astray, lose them, and return later for us.'

Her husband groaned again as he moved slightly.

'Ay — Waleran was born near here — he knows the forest hood blind.'

Emma could sense that his hand was now feeling for the dagger. He heaved a sigh of relief as his fingers touched it.

'So we are to spend the hours of daylight hidden, here, in the darkness. So be it — I only hope the entrance is well hidden.'

'Well, no,' Emma faltered — 'But no one can tell from the forest track that there is a shaft here. The slope just drops down from the middle of a small grassy field. No one would think of a mine being here if they had no knowledge of it.'

Sir Berengar tried to sit up, swore again, and laid his head and shoulders back on his wife's lap.

'Try to sleep, it will ease your head,' she murmured.

He gave a little contented grunt, sighed,

and relaxed against her — but he did not fall asleep yet. His hands crept insistently back to her waist and up over her breast.

Her arms were still out of the gown's sleeves. She had left struggling back into them, and had left the retying of the neck strings until she could do so without jolting her husband.

His hands explored the bare arm and shoulder, found the neck string of her shift, tugged the bow loose and slid the shift down over her shoulders.

He wriggled his shoulders higher against her, felt his way to grasp her hair, and pulled her head down towards him.

'Kiss me' — an order.

Emma bent to where his hand feebly but insistently guided her head, and kissed him, with fluttering lips — quickly and lightly, a girl's kiss.

'No,' he said. 'As a woman kisses.'

Emma bent again and met his demanding mouth. He held her in a long exploratory kiss.

Satisfied, he let her free, sighed sleepily, turned his face against her breast, rubbed his cheek appreciatively against the naked skin, nuzzled until his mouth found the nipple and tugged at it gently as he drifted into sleep.

Emma pulled the cloak over both of them

as her husband slept. She felt strangely protective.

She must have slept for a short time although she had tried to keep alert.

Emma felt two fingers laid over her lips as she returned to wakefulness.

Somewhere a vixen was screaming — that peculiar strangled cry — a pause — and the same cry again — for longer. A pause — this time the cry had a broken note in it, cut short.

Sir Berengar's fingers gripped her wrist. The cry of a dog fox came from his lips.

'Waleran,' he breathed.

Emma heard no footstep approach the shaft but suddenly there was a whining squeak from the entrance to the mine answered by a double whine from beside her.

Then the presence of Waleran was with them, whispering news of his exploits.

He had, he said, after a few circuitous miles, led his pursuers away from the mine, given Gerold and his men the slip, lain low until darkness came, then returned by another way. He had hidden the horses among the trees.

He helped Sir Berengar to his feet, supported him out of the shaft, and held him up, in a stumbling walk to the shelter of a thick copse where the horses were hidden.

There was a whispered consultation between the two men.

Emma heard the words 'Geddington' and 'Safe.'

14

They mounted quietly and set off as quickly as possible down the track towards Stanion. They did not go through the village, but circled it to rejoin the track to Geddington.

'Once we reach there we shall be safe. At Geddington is the King's Hunting Lodge. The castellan is well known to me,' explained Sir Berengar.

Emma looked puzzled — this was moving in high places indeed.

Her husband replied almost apologetically, 'I am near in age to the Lord Edward. As a boy I was called upon to bear him company at the hunt whenever King Henry came to Geddington. I rode with the Lord Edward, hawked, and coursed the hare.'

Emma determined to ask more about King Henry III and his eldest son, the Lord Edward, when opportunity arose.

Her horse's stride lengthened again. She watched the shadows beside the track. She was expecting an ambush from behind every oak that loomed up beside the track — but none came.

Instead the trees began to thin. The moon

came out from behind a cloud.

Sir Berengar's face was strained. He was clutching his horse's mane to keep upright.

Emma could now see the outline of a church upon a gently rising knoll; the silvery streak of the small river Ise beyond; a pack horse bridge over the river; and behind the church the timber brattice which enclosed the hunting palace of King Henry III.

The brattice, a palisade of pointed timber baulks, fastened solidly side by side, was sixteen feet high.

Set in the brattice was a stone gatehouse, with its large entrance archway, at present closed and barred by two great solidly built timber gates.

The stonework on either side of the entrance arch had no windows and presented a blank stone face to any attack.

Above the arch and extending to either side were living quarters for the constable.

Beyond the gatehouse Emma could just discern the roofs, tiled with oak shingles, of the King's greenwood palace — the chapel, the hall, the bakehouse, brewhouse, granary, dairy, kitchen, dovecote and a jumble of roofs beyond.

Waleran had no need to set up a clamour, for the alaunts left to roam at will within the huge enclosure at night had already warned of their approach.

The shutter was withdrawn from a narrow slit window into the room above the arch, and they were inspected closely by its occupant.

A peremptory order to state their names and business followed.

Waleran gave his master's name and the fact that he was sorely hurt, which was evident from the way he was slumped over his horse's neck again.

Waleran begged shelter for the night for Sir Berengar and his newly wedded wife, the Lady Emma.

The face disappeared, much shouting ensued, the gates swung open to allow the visitors to ride through, and were immediately closed and barred behind them.

Sir William Caunville, the King's constable at Geddington, stood to receive his guests, backed by four of his stalwart retainers.

The four soon lifted Sir Berengar from his horse, and at a word from Sir William carried him up the newel stair to the solar over the arch.

A pallet of straw was hastily put down on the floor and covered by a sheet, then Emma's husband was lowered carefully on to it.

He was only just conscious but he managed to murmur his thanks.

More candles were lit, by whose flickering light the blood soaked bandage across her husband's forehead was plainly visible.

Emma explained quickly that the wound had not been properly washed.

Sir William at once sent for a bowl of water, clean linen and a jar of wine.

When the men had finished going over her husband's limp form for signs of broken bones or other serious injury they nodded to Sir William and stood aside.

Great weals and bruises almost covered the top half of their patient.

They had stripped off Sir Berengar's garments down to the braies cloth.

'Bruises only — and the head wound,' said Sir William. 'Your man is capable?'

'Very capable, and experienced,' replied Emma, as Waleran knelt opposite to her and began to soak the bandage to soften the congealed blood, then gently drew it away from the wound.

Emma tore off a fresh piece of linen for each swab until the long cut was clean, poured on wine, then bandaged it afresh.

The four men lifted Sir Berengar carefully and put him between the sheets of the big bed, drawing up the covers. They then left the solar.

Sir William was kindness itself. He sent for

refreshment of bread and meat and wine.

'Be of good cheer lady. A few days rest will see my old friend as good as new. You are both to have the use of this room until Sir Berengar is well enough to travel.'

Emma thanked him, blinking a little, for tears of reaction had come into her eyes.

He bade Waleran go below where the men would find him food and a bed.

'The horses have been stabled while you attended to your master,' continued Sir William.

His 'goodnight,' was gruff but kindly.

Emma stood by the bed and regarded the unconscious figure on it, then pulled up a joint stool and prepared to watch through the night.

She leaned over to tuck the covers more closely over her husband's shoulders.

Tears splashed on to his face.

He moved slightly. There was a groan as his eyes opened, and, as blinking, he tried to focus his gaze, first on the candle, then on his wife's face.

His mouth twisted in a wry smile as recognition came.

Emma held a cup of wine to his lips, sliding her arm round his shoulders to raise his head against her shoulder as he drank thirstily.

'Where are we?'

'Safe within the brattices of Geddington. There is no need for you to stir. Sir William bids you rest until you have recovered and are well enough to ride to Bernewelle le Moyne.'

Sir Berengar clasped his wife's hand in a groping hold so that she could not draw back without jolting him.

'So be it, lady.'

His other hand explored the bandage. He winced as it reached the pad over the gash.

His wife lowered him carefully down to the pillow again.

Petulantly — 'I'm as weak as a new born lamb!'

'It is the loss of blood — you will feel stronger even by the morning.'

He frowned, then sighed resignedly, and let his gaze roam around the room.

'Where do you sleep?'

'I stay here and watch out the remainder of the night.'

His gaze rested on the straw pallet, left on the floor.

The shadow of his former commanding glare crossed his face. His grasp tightened.

'You'll do as you are bid, and sleep in comfort in this bed.'

Emma's chin went up.

Her husband began painfully to roll over, in preparation for getting up.

Emma's capitulation followed swiftly.

Anything was better than causing his wound to bleed afresh.

She trod lightly round to the other side of the bed, untied her gown and undergown, slid them down quickly, stepped out of them, retaining the white shift. She tossed the gowns over the clothes perch and drew back the corner of the coverlets. She took off her shoes and hose.

Her gaze met her husband's quizzical look and she felt colour flooding into her cheeks.

Laughter lines were crinkling the corner of his eyes. He whispered in an amused tone, 'Lie between the blankets, Kyndel, lest you tempt the lamb to break his word to your father.'

15

Long before her husband woke Emma was up and sitting by the window embrasure, with the wooden shutters drawn back.

The noise of the gates being opened had roused her to activity.

She watched with amazement the arrival of the King's baggage train as it came across the packhorse bridge, from the south, past the few tofts of the village, and went under the arch beneath her viewpoint.

There was a string of packhorses with their attendants. There were the packhorses of the chamberlains. There were the packhorses of each officer of the King's household. Each was marked by its owner's colourful livery.

Emma puzzled over the shape, wrapped in canvas, of one large bundle which was strapped to a beautifully groomed horse adorned by the King's livery, until Sir Berengar rolled from the bed, draped himself in a blanket, and joined her by the window.

'It is the King's bed,' he pointed out, 'There is a second horse carrying the sheets and furs. The third horse carries the hangings which can transform an ordinary room into the likeness of a palace.'

After the last pack horse had gone from sight Emma guiltily turned away from the window. There was work to be done before the arrival of the Royal party later in the day.

Her husband's bandages needed changing. Their clothing needed to be brushed and mended.

In the event they had plenty of time. The Royal party was not expected until much later in the day.

After Emma and her husband had broken their fast Sir Berengar spoke to Sir William and asked his permission to enter one of the King's chapels to render thanks to God for their deliverance.

Sir William was delighted that his protégé was feeling well enough to get up, dress and eat.

He readily gave permission, and in addition suggested that they used the time before the King's arrival to visit the Royal Mews.

Sir Berengar and Emma had been given permission to pray in the largest of the three chapels.

One was the Queen's own chapel, one was a small chapel for the King's use, built in the oriel over the doorway to his chamber.

The third chapel had a pentice covered way leading from it to the cloister by the hall.

Sir Berengar and his lady left the gatehouse, skirted the large hall, entered the cloister by the wall of the hall and walked along under the pentice roofing to the chapel door.

An usher opened the door; they entered.

Emma stood still for a moment, absorbing the impression of green painted wainscotting studded with gold stars, the painted screen in front of the chancel, the glass in the high windows.

Drawing nearer to the altar husband and wife knelt in prayer.

They paced slowly back from the chapel, along the pentice, through the cloisters and past the end of the spacious timber hall.

Some of its windows had oiled linen cloth to cover them, some had glass.

Emma looked curiously at the windows that held glass, for she had never seen a glass window before that day.

Catching Sir Berengar's eye on her she tried to look disinterested, as though such luxury was everyday commonplace in her life — then smiled and admitted to curiosity.

'How is it made?'

Emma suddenly realised on looking closely at her husband that he was finding it an effort to appear as tireless as usual.

She promptly wilted.

'May we sit for a while? The night's journey has tired me.'

He led her over to a heap of canvas wrapped bales of hangings, unloaded from the pack horses, but not yet carried into the hall.

He moved the bales, arranging two to form a low seat, with the rest of the pile behind them for a back and head rest.

He handed Emma to the seat and then sat down himself, leaning his shoulders and head against the higher bales.

Emma congratulated herself on her strategy, and prepared to look wan and exhausted for a long time.

Sir Berengar narrowed his eyes against the sun, glanced up at the circular window and began, 'The window began as a mixture of sand, potash and lime . . . ' His voice then went on through the process of heating the mixture in clay containers — and on — and on — to the glass being molten — and on to blowing a bubble of glass — and on to the bullion mark left behind, called a 'bull's eye'.

He finished with, 'But the King's glass is made in England now — look — you can see the 'bull's eye' mark in the centre, left by the pontil of Laurence Vitrearius.'

Sir Berengar stood up, flexing his shoulder muscles, and held out his hand to Emma.

'You have led me into resting my hurt for long enough. Come, let us inspect the King's falcons. It would be tactful to find some good specimens to praise to his royal person.'

Emma was satisfied. The white shade had gone from his face. The rest had done its work.

They walked back round the hall to the opposite end, where a pentice extended to the kitchen on the leeward side of the hall.

They continued past a cluster of buildings, the granary, the brewhouse, the bakehouse, the entrance to the dog court, past the dove cote and on to the mews — an extensive range of timber hutments — for most of the royal hawks were kept there.

Here, their guide, Edgar, was waiting for them.

Spaced out all over the grass were perches — block perches, ring perches, bow perches and triangular perches.

Peregrines were on the block perches, goshawks on the ring and bow perches.

They watched a falconer move an empty block perch, pulling its spike out of the ground by tugging at the cylinder shaped piece of wood to which it was fixed.

Then he moved it to a clean patch of grass and knocked it into the ground with a mallet.

Edgar pointed to another falconer who was bringing a shallow tub of water. He put it on the grass beside the block on which perched a peregrine.

The peregrine stepped into the bath and began to splash the water over his head and back. His leash was long enough to allow him plenty of freedom to splash and it was fastened to a separate stake of wood beside the block.

Edgar guided Sir Berengar and the Lady Emma, very quietly into the weathering shed, then into the shed for peregrines who were almost fully trained.

On their way to the 'hacking' ground they passed two falconers, each carrying a goshawk on the gloved left fist.

Neither goshawk wore a hood. They were being accustomed to being carried.

16

From afar off came the sound of a trumpet.

Emma looked up at her husband. He nodded.

'It is the King's company. We'll make our way to the gatehouse.'

By the time the long cavalcade had reached the stone packhorse bridge Sir Berengar and the Lady Emma were in position, a little way behind Sir William Cauneville and his retinue of welcome.

Emma had never seen so much moving colour. The cavalcade seemed a long, sinuous line of intermingling blue, scarlet, yellow, green, black, red, grey, yellow-brown, tawny, greenish blue watchet, purple red murrey and reddish brown, with touches of gold and silver.

It wound over the bridge and came on towards the gatehouse, and under the gatehouse arch to the courtyard.

Sir William knelt in front of a resplendent figure mounted on a fine chestnut horse. This must be the king.

Emma looked with absorbed interest at his long tunic of deep purple red, at his mantle, lined with sable, at the silver mountings of his horse's harness.

He was a man well advanced in age — about fifty at a guess, with greying hair and some excess weight!

Emma counted rapidly. He had been born in 1207 and it was now 1258 so he must be fifty one years old.

The haute lady beside him must be his Queen, Eleanor of Provence.

The Queen wore a full skirted gown of scarlet, with close fitting long sleeves and a fairly low, round neckline.

Round her head she wore a crown-like circlet of linen. Her hair was arranged in large coils on either side of her head.

Over the coils she wore the barbette, the band of linen passing under the chin and over the head beneath the circlet.

A girdle of gold clasped the waist of the gown, the two free ends hanging nearly to the hem of it.

Emma's glance travelled to the figure behind the dismounting Royal Henry III.

This man was much younger, about nineteen, a straight, commanding figure.

When he swung to the ground Emma beheld a tall, powerfully built man, broad of chest, with long arms and legs.

His hair was flaxen. His head was flung

back; he was running a quick, all embracing glance over the assembled company.

His glance flickered over Sir Berengar and a look of surprise and pleasure dawned momentarily.

Then his left eyelid drooped again as he acknowledged in his turn the greetings of Sir William Caunville.

Emma's interest veered to the person of a very young lady, standing behind the Queen. Who could she be?

She was about thirteen years old — younger than Emma.

She was very beautiful, with a slightly olive skin and dark hair. Her gown was of light blue fustian, silky looking like velvet. Her glance followed the every movement of the tall commanding man, with pride and adoration.

Sir Berengar followed Emma's glance and whispered, 'The young man is the Lord Edward, the King's eldest son; the young lady is his child-bride, Eleanor of Castile. They were married four years ago at Burgos when he was but fifteen.'

Emma looked again.

No wonder the people nicknamed the Lord Edward 'Longshanks'.

He stood a head taller than most other men, her husband excepted.

But even he was not quite as tall as the Lord Edward.

Emma considered thoughtfully — they were somewhat alike, the same straight look, the same air of confidence, much the same age, but of very different degree, fortunately for Emma.

The kaleidoscope of colour continued on its way — the King's officers of the wardrobe, his almoner, his chamberlains. All passed beneath the arch; all with their own servants in colourful livery.

Here and there Emma recognised the badge of a family whose name was a household word.

When all had dispersed to their various quarters Sir Berengar and Emma returned to the gatehouse solar to make ready for the midday meal in the great hall.

A page arrived bearing a message from the Lord Edward. It summoned Sir Berengar to his private chamber after the meal was over.

Sir Berengar and Lady Emma entered the hall in good time and stood by their designated bench, waiting for the arrival of the King.

The high table had two canopied, carved, and painted chairs for the King and Queen. Set in the wall above the canopied chairs

122

were the two circular glass windows, each with its bullion centre.

Emma looked down to the bottom of the hall where the spear draught shield projections ran out from the wall and almost joined a central moveable screen across the bottom end.

Two gaps were left for service, also a central gap through which one reached the pentice leading to the timber kitchen outside.

The screens and draught spears formed a passageway.

Above the level of the wooden screens was another clear glass window, with the image of the king set in glass.

The high table at the top of the 'U' shape was for the King and his immediate family. All his chamberlains and officers of his household would sit down either side of one of the arms of the 'U'.

There were timber pillars down each side of the hall, holding up the roof trees and forming two aisles on either side of the main space.

Rich drapings had been hung at various points around the walls of the hall, the self same hangings Emma guessed she had seen as rolls on a pack horse's back.

The walls themselves were painted in a tempera type of colour.

King Henry III entered from a doorway behind the high table.

He was leading his Queen and was followed by the tall, purposeful figure of Lord Edward.

The King's chaplain did his part; those at the high table sat when the King sat, and lesser mortals followed suit.

Emma was engrossed for some minutes in watching the chattering, changing scene, then pulled herself together to converse and play her part as the responsible quick witted wife of a knight — lowly but by no means to be despised.

Quips were being aimed at her husband from an old acquaintance a few places up the table, one Eustache de la Haache.

'Remember the day the Lord Edward drew his sword on you?'

Sir Berengar laughed — 'Ay — I must have been all of seventeen.'

Sir Eustache explained for the benefit of suddenly quiet neighbours at table.

'Lord Edward was hawking with Sir Berengar, one on either side of a small river. Sir Berengar made a mistake with the falcon — the Lord Edward lost his temper and a hail of words was shouted at Sir Berengar. Whereupon Sir Berengar replied to the Lord Edward's threats — 'It's just as well the stream divides us.' So the Lord Edward turned his horse, plunged into the stream, reached the other side and pursued Sir Berengar with his drawn sword. Sir Berengar wisely refrained from resistance, the prince let him go and they both shook with laugher.'

There was laughter again, at Sir Eustache's efforts at mimicry.

When the meal was finished the King retired to his chamber to attend to State business.

Sir Berengar was conducted to the Lord Edward's chamber by a page, and another page escorted the Lady Emma to the gatehouse solar.

Some time later her husband returned, looking deeply pleased, and confident.

'Sir William has told the Lord Edward of our hurried marriage, the affray and our desperate struggle to reach the shelter of Geddington. He has promised to lend me an escort of five men to see us on our way to Bernewelle le Moyne, and to send two of his men to make enquiries at Weldon for our missing retainers and horses.'

The missing retainers duly arrived later in the day — in the train of Sir Osborne Loval, the Master of the Royal Buckhounds, who lived a short distance out of Weldon at

Hunter's Manor, and had been summoned to the King's presence.

Loval held the Manor in Little Weldon known as Hunter's Manor, by the service of keeping certain hounds of the King's pack, and attending his sovereign when he came to hunt in Rockingham Forest.

Sir Berengar restored his two somewhat battered retainers to Waleran's charge, with orders for the refurbishing of their raiment.

Waleran examined the rescued horses and their baggage and pronounced the contents complete and undamaged.

17

For the evening meal, and entertainment, Sir Berengar and the Lady Emma could now appear dressed in more suitable raiment than the grass stained garments they now wore.

Emma's husband gave orders that his three men were to put on their reserve clothing bearing the Le Moyne arms.

They would attend his progress to the great hall and take up their position with the retainers of the great.

The Lady Emma longed at this point to suggest that her energetic partner would do well to lie down to rest for the remaining hours until the evening festivities.

Glancing at his bandages she took breath to say so, gulped and remained silent.

She guessed what the stinging reply would be, and turned away.

Waleran had followed Emma's glance.

Left with Sir Berengar he gruffly echoed Emma's unspoken question about the gash and was told curtly that it was but a scratch.

Waleran had one great advantage over the Lady Emma. He had served his master's father.

He proceeded to give a pithy description of the agonies of Sir Renaud's last hours, all due apparently, to the disregarding of Waleran's good advice on the care of a wound.

Waleran prevailed, where Emma would have been scorned.

Her husband retired to the gatehouse solar and flung himself, grumbling, on to the bed.

Emma silently half closed the shutters. In a very short space of time Sir Berengar was fast asleep.

Sitting by the half closed shutters Emma's plans for the evening were soon made. The gown of light greenish blue watchet; it would need to be.

Excitement began to rise in her. Surely there would be a goodly feast for the eyes — a tumbler, a jongleur, maybe even dancing.

Quietly Emma made preparation while Sir Berengar still slept.

Later their progress across the courtyard to the Great Hall was dignified by the attendance of a sprucely garbed Waleran, Turold, and Segar, each bearing on his tunic the badge of Le Moyne, argent a cross paty gules — on a silver/white background, a red cross, the arms spreading out diagonally into wide flanges.

Emma glanced surreptitiously at her husband.

He wore a long tunic to the ankles. The tunic was slit up the front, level with the thighs. The sleeves were wide at the shoulder, but narrowed down to a small cuff at the wrist.

At every stride the tunic swirled a little way open.

It was belted at the waist with an ornate girdle that had one long, hanging end at the centre.

A glow of pride surged through Emma.

Her own gown was long and full, laced tightly to the figure at the back.

The sleeves were long and fitted closely. Emma also wore a girdle, ending in a long hanging strap from the centre waist.

She had coiled her plaits round her ears, wound the linen barbette under her chin and over her head, and put on the circlet of linen.

There was an air of suppressed tumult and excitement in the hall.

Sir Berengar and the Lady Emma stood talking to Sir Eustache de la Haache until the King and Queen and their immediate retinue approached the high table.

The King wore a purple supertunic which hung free from the shoulders to the ankle.

The sleeves were very wide and long, and gathered into small pleats on the shoulder.

There was a short slit in the front of each sleeve so that the arms could pass through, leaving the sleeve hanging loose to the knee.

Prayers were recited. The King and Queen sat down. Everyone followed suit.

The King then spoke to his master of ceremonies.

The subtlety, a compliment to the King, was carried in first and placed upon the centre of the white linen cloth, in front of him.

Upon the silver charger were the figures of the King's two favourite saints — St Mary and St John, made of sugar and paste and decorated in glowing colours.

A figure of a crowned King stood between the saints. They each had a hand raised in benediction.

The subtlety was to be viewed, not eaten.

Behind it came a procession of attendants each carrying a large dish upon which lay one of the choice foods of the first course.

There was venison with furmenty, Boar's head, with tusks, roast pork, custard pie.

The subtlety which heralded the arrival of the second course was in the form of an eagle wearing a coronet of gold.

For that course there was roast crane, roast heron, glazed chicken, bream and tarts.

The third course was preceded by a subtlety of a woodland scene, with figures on horseback riding through the wood, each with a falcon on a gloved hand.

The third course included roast venison, hare stewed with chives, roast quail, roast lark, small loaves and fritters.

Platters of meat were being carried from behind the screens at the bottom end of the hall; pitchers of wine were being poured; the hubbub of voices began to rise — then on a sustained note from a gittern three tumbling figures jumped from behind the draught shield projection at the end of the hall and came rolling head over heels to the centre of the floor space.

The acrobats seemed to be made of dough.

They stood on their hands, walked on their hands, somersaulted back to a standing position, made a pyramid for one to climb and stand on the shoulders of the others.

The topmost then stood on his hands, using the heads of his companions as a base.

When their turn finished they stood bowing before the King and Queen and company, then collected up the scattered coins tossed by the audience, and retired behind the screens.

Two figures emerged and walked to the centre of the floor, a man and a woman, the man holding a rebec and a stool.

He put down his stool, mounted one foot on it and played a note on the rebec.

The woman began to sing, holding a flower in her fingers, looking at it, pretending she had not noticed the man.

The second song went on for forty five verses, following which the two performers, after much bowing retired.

From behind the screens musicians came forward, bowing. They took up their position and, at a word from a chamberlain began the music for a dance.

The king rose and led Queen Eleanor to the space in the centre of the floor.

The Lord Edward followed, smiling down at his wife, the Lady Eleanor.

Most of their suite followed, until they were spaced in an oval shape of dancers around the fire tiles in the centre of the hall.

Each lady stood by her gentleman, side by side, holding inside hands without raising the arms.

Emma watched with intense interest, counting the steps and memorising the sequence.

She could dance the farandole, running

madly, or walking sedately; everyone could. It was often danced on the green, then winding round the tofts of the village, danced to the singing of the performers.

Emma's gaze followed, not Queen Eleanor of Provence, but the Lord Edward's young wife, the Lady Eleanor of Castile.

Her face was radiant. She performed her part with such supple grace; her slim figure inclining to the slow walking movement of the dance.

Every step was precise. One hand held up the skirt of her gown.

Emma felt the conscious arching of her foot as she made each beautifully timed slow movement, felt her joy at being at one with the music, exactly in time.

Her eyes were shining with the pleasure of the dance and no doubt also with the joy of her hand being held in her adored Lord Edward's grasp.

For Emma had gathered from court gossip that the young princess was but thirteen years of age.

When the dance finished the dancers joined hands in a circle for a round dance.

When that dance finished the King and Queen went back to the high table.

This seemed to be the signal for the occupants of the side tables to join the dancers if they so wished.

Emma felt Sir Berengar's hand under her elbow, urging her to rise, and she looked questioningly up at him.

There was a smile lurking in his eyes.

'I feel sure you know the pattern of steps of a Branle.'

Her reply was stammered in some confusion, 'Y-yes, I think so. I have tried the steps in the empty brew house with Emelota at home,' — and wondered if he could have guessed that she was longing to join the dancers.

He was incredibly good in the dance, giving Emma's hand an unseen tug if she seemed to hesitate for direction.

He also seemed filled with secret joy, his eyes crinkling at the corners and his mouth curving in an amused smile.

As the dancing finished and they were returning to the table, Emma thanked him shyly for his help but forbore to mention that she had not expected him to be so accomplished.

Her husband laughed outright. 'I learned many years ago to take my part in the dance — for as one of the companions of the Lord Edward on his visits here I was at the King's command afterwards in the hall. Many times at his direction I have partnered a noble lady who wished to dance.'

Emma took breath to ask him if he had ever aspired to the hand of one of these ladies — but recollected in time that it was not a suitable question for a 'meek and obedient' new wife.

Sir Berengar looked down at Emma.

'No,' he said, 'I did not.'

It was uncanny.

18

The following morning sped by with the endless coming and going of the members of the King's entourage.

The King and the Lord Edward inspected the mews in the morning, hearing much of what Sir Berengar and the Lady Emma had heard during their progress through the enclosure the previous day.

The afternoon was devoted to falconry by the King and his party.

Sir Berengar and the Lady Emma rode at the tail end of the group.

'I wish you could see the Lord Edward's performance at a tourney,' remarked Sir Berengar. 'He has travelled through Gascony and Guienne during the years since his marriage, taking part in many affrays with his knights. Not individual jousting but a mass conflict of side against side, which is very like real war.'

'Why do they take such risks when not actually taking part in a real war?' asked Emma.

'It is training for war,' replied Sir Berengar. 'Sometimes there is a clash between thirty or forty knights on each side. William the Marshal gained fame throughout the continent by his skill in such a tournament.'

'Have you taken part in a tournament?' questioned Emma.

'A fair number,' he laughed.

The Lord Edward heard the laughter, turned, and rode over to accompany them for some of the way.

Sir Berengar continued, 'Sire do you remember the tournament at Blyth in '56 to mark your debut when you were seventeen?'

The Lord Edward grinned. 'When we fought in cloth armour with light arms — blunted! But the tournament grew rougher. I remember the older men with torn muscles — William Longespe, Roger Bigod, the Earl Marshall, Roger de Quince, the Earl of Winchester and two judges, Alan de Watsand and John of Lexington who never fully recovered.'

The Lord Edward frowned in remembrance. 'Trouble came from the quarrelsome squires — and the footmen and spectators who got out of hand.'

'Now, how does your wound heal? Do you feel fit enough to accompany me this evening? I have been chosen as 'Master of

Game' for the hunt tomorrow and wish to sound out the ground tonight to ensure a good day's hunting in the morning.'

A flush of pleasure crept up over Sir Berengar's cheeks.

He accepted the invitation with alacrity, denying at once that his hurt pained him at all.

The Lord Edward then rode back to his wife's side, gerfalcon on gloved fist.

He was a superb horseman, his length of limb giving him an advantage.

They rode on towards Monk's Wood where kites breed freely.

Sir Berengar glanced thoughtfully at his wife. 'The king believes kite hawking to be the ultimate test of falconry. Have you ever seen gerfalcons stoop to a kite?'

Emma shook her head.

'I thought not — then I had better warn you that a decoy — a tame eagle owl, with a fox's brush tied to its jesses, will be used to lure the kites down from flying at their usual great height. The kites think that the fox's brush is prey carried by the Eagle Owl.

'As soon as a kite is nearly down to the level of the Eagle Owl the King will 'strike the hood' and cast off his gerfalcon — so will the Lord Edward — and the two gerfalcons will work together, gain height, and stoop to catch the kite.'

Emma thanked her Lord for warning her.

She could not help being glad that they were at the tail end of the riders and would providentially miss a close view of the kill.

During the meal that evening the subtlety was of a woodland scene — a hart feeding, a lymerer and his leashed scenting hound — the lymerer in the colours of the King's livery.

For the first course the company enjoyed fillets of pork in galantine, Viand Royal, cygnets, capon and small pies.

The subtlety preceding the second course was of the hunt in progress.

There was a choice of venison with furmenty, suckling pigs, Mallard duck, roast bittern, stuffed chicken, partridges, fried slices, brawn in pepper sauce.

The third subtlety was of a woodland scene — a hart at bay facing a victorious hunter — the crowned figure of a king.

This was followed by cream of almonds, pears in syrup, roast venison, roast kid, roast woodcock, plover, quails, snipe, fieldfare, and fritters.

During the meal Sir Berengar seemed interested in a stranger, one particular knight who was sitting farther up the table.

He questioned Sir Eustache de la Haache, who was sitting beside Sir Berengar on the other side from Emma.

The unknown knight appeared to be about twenty years old, dark, good looking, self assured.

In answer to Sir Berengar's question 'Who is he?' Sir Eustache replied.

'He is Sir Otho de Grandison and is a newcomer to the Lord Edward's retinue this year. He is performing the duties of a secretary.'

'Where does he hail from?' continued Sir Berengar.

'From Savoy as does Queen Eleanor. Sir Otho is one of the six sons of Count Peter de Grandison, who has recently died. Count Peter of Savoy, Queen Eleanor's uncle, was his protector. Count Peter of Savoy offered to take three of the fatherless sons to England with him, in his service, on his visit here this year. The Lord Edward quickly recognises men of great ability and gathers round him those of about his own age.'

Emma smiled, 'So he 'gathered' Sir Otho?'

'And a very welcome addition he is,' commented her husband.

That evening Sir Berengar accompanied the Lord Edward to the meeting of the huntsmen, over which he presided.

The Lord Edward had already warned the sergeant, the leaders of hounds, and the lymerers.

As 'The Master of Game', he had already decided where in the forest the gathering was to take place.

Leaving nothing to chance he was going to take his huntsmen quietly to find deer feeding, ready for the hunt in the morning.

He had learned as a boy to recognise from the size of 'slot' prints whether the hart would be large enough — 'A hart of ten,' and therefore chaceable.

19

The hunting party rose well before dawn, and soon after daybreak were riding through the oak woods to Pedlar's Wells, the gathering place chosen by the Lord Edward.

The Lord Edward had teasingly commanded Sir Berengar to restrain his ardour for the chase and guide his newly wedded wife's inexperienced woodcraft.

He knew that Emma had not attended a Royal Assembly before.

Everything was prepared as he had ordered at the discussion the previous evening.

White linen cloths were spread upon the grass. Platters of cold roast meats were laid upon the cloths — roast beef, roast lamb, roast kid, pork stuffed with sage, capon, hare, woodcock, quail, plover, heron, peacock, swan, crane — and fish — salmon, trout, perch, roach, eels, pike and iced hard boiled eggs.

Grooms took the horses as everyone dismounted. Sir Berengar and the Lady Emma joined a lively, laughing group sitting round a cloth, Sir Eustache de la Haache among them.

Emma watched as she began to eat. She saw the lymerers and huntsmen, one after the other, come up to the Lord Edward (who was standing with his own huntsman) and make his report of what he had done and seen.

Each huntsman held his horn and shook out the contents into his hand — the droppings of the hart he had found in the forest.

The Master of Game inspected each offering carefully, then called one man back, handing him over to the care of his own huntsman.

Evidently this lymerer's hart was judged to be the greatest.

When the meal was ended more orders were given. The huntsmen with their couples of hounds dispersed to their appointed places in the wood — judged by the Master of Game to be the most likely places where the hart would run, and ready to be unleashed as he went by.

Then everyone was mounted and ready to ride. The Master of Game, and the lymerer with his scenting hound, went to where the huntsman had seen evidence of the hart of ten, followed by a huntsman holding the leashes of the coupled hounds.

When the hart was seen the lymerer blew a long note on his horn — and a recheat — and the huntsman uncoupled his hounds.

Everyone rode towards the sound of the horn, knowing from its notes that the hart had been sighted.

Once Sir Berengar had to hold Emma's rein while they waited for the scent to be found again.

The hart had gone back upon his own track for a little way and then changed direction.

Soon they came to a stream. The hounds checked and began to sniff around.

Emma and her husband watched as the huntsman went downstream for the hounds to find the scent — no luck — then upstream.

Emma was hoping that the hart had managed to go far enough upstream to lose the hounds, but one old hound found the scent — and the chase went on.

Sir Berengar unaccountably checked his horse's pace.

Emma followed suit and let the rest of the hunt, led by the King, go past.

Sir Berengar glanced at her ruefully.

'Guard your demeanour well, the hart is nearly spent, soon he will turn at bay.'

Again he had read Emma's thoughts. It would not be seemly to show a shrinking countenance at the King's hunt, however bloody the end.

In the event it was a quick end for the hart.

He stood at bay facing his pursuers, in the middle of a green glade. He was a noble animal — a hart of ten.

He was killed by a sword thrust behind the shoulder to the heart.

As they were leaving the glade, after the customary ritual, Sir Berengar complimented the Lord Edward on the events of the day.

The Prince was naturally pleased that he had performed his duties so adroitly in front of his father, the King.

'You shall have Ancel, my huntsman, to entertain you during the time before we break bread. I will send him to you well before that time. He will recite 'The Nature of the Hart' for you. He is well versed; it will amuse your Lady.'

Emma thanked him shyly.

They did not hurry, but rode easily to Geddington, with much chatter and laughter among the small groups riding together.

Ancel, the huntsman, duly presented himself, holding the 'head' of a hart of ten in his hands.

Sir Berengar leaned against the window embrasure comfortably, while Emma perched on the 'X' stool to hear the huntsman's words.

He began, 'The hart is a common beast enough . . . '

He continued with the hart's cunning, the hart's rut, the hart's bellowing during the rut, the hart's shedding of horns in the month of March.

The audience of two listened politely to the life story — from the day a calf was born to his fifth year — of being a stag — to his sixth year when he is a hart of ten and chaceable.

The saga continued through to various types of droppings, and the wisdom of an old deer — how he uses rivers and pools to put the hounds off the scent.

At last the huntsman's voice stopped. The huntsman bowed — evidently the recital was over.

Sir Berengar held out his hand, expressed thanks for the huntsman's dissertation, and dropped a silver coin into his palm.

He went out, clutching the antlers with which he had illustrated his talk.

Sir Berengar's shoulders were still propped against the window embrasure. He glanced across at his wife, his eyes full of merriment.

He emitted a realistic bellow, straightened, and took a step towards her.

Emma hastily dodged behind the stool, and waited, laughter breaking through, but

146

eyeing her husband apprehensively.

He chuckled, then bellowed with increased realism.

Emma backed away warily, a step at a time, trying not to look as nervous as she felt, as he side stepped the stool and came towards her.

Still retreating, Emma felt the barrier of the bed behind her.

Sir Berengar's face lit up. He smiled impishly.

Emma turned, fleeing round the end of the bed, to be stopped by a pair of strong arms flung round her, a mouth nuzzling the back of her neck, and a playful nip on the shoulder.

Her husband pretended to worry Emma in his teeth as a hound shakes a hare, and then turned her to face him.

Suddenly the laughter died out of his face; his hold strengthened. He was regarding Emma intently, his face serious.

Then his arms tightened and with an inarticulate sound he pulled her against his suddenly taut body, and his mouth closed down on hers with a desperate hunger.

'Jesus,' he whispered, 'We cannot attain Bernewelle too speedily for my content.'

Smiling again he adroitly placed one foot behind Emma's heels and capsized her flat on her back across the bed.

Shaking his head in mock reproof he murmured, 'You should have been ready for such a move.'

'I haven't had your . . . ' and Emma bit back the rest of the retort.

He joined her, lying face down by her side, one arm flung across her waist.

'Practice? — or should it be experience? — Diote? — You were right about her. Silver was what she craved. Silver bought her manumission.'

Emma frowned in the effort of recollection.

The chapman had said as much — but how did her husband know that she had commented on it?

He chuckled, nipped Emma's shoulder gently and licked the place better.

She tried to turn to see his face but his arm across her waist held her flat.

'Who told you of it?'

He clicked his tongue in astonishment.

'You would have me betray my sources of information? No, no, a good commander keeps his sources of intelligence to himself.'

Emma jerked round under his suddenly slack arm — straight into a bear hug that smothered further questions for some considerable time.

Sir Berengar and the Lady Emma had to

hurry to reach the hall that evening before the arrival of the King and his entourage.

Today the subtleties were again of falconry — for the next day the King was due to ride towards a heronry to try his skill at heron hawking.

The first course had a Cockatrice for the chief dish — the forward part of a capon sewn to the hind part of a pig, and the forward part of the pig and hind part of the capon also sewn together, then roasted and glazed.

Stuffed pork, shoulder of mutton, and potted meat were easily recognisable.

The second course had venison, roast kid, roast heron, pigeons and hare.

The third course consisted of cream of Almonds, pears in syrup, tench, trout, perch, roast eel and lamprey.

Emma lay awake that night; sleep would not come to her.

Turning restlessly to the other side for the fifth time she sensed a tenseness from the apparently sleeping form at the far edge of the bed.

'What troubles you Kyndel?'

'Bernewelle,' Emma faltered. It was but a fraction of the truth.

He sat up with a jerk.

'So?'

'You seem to be receding farther and farther away, the other things are growing and growing the nearer the ceremony approaches — things like the time worn customs, the public bedding, the usual pleasantries. I know it is customary, I know it is even politic — for I'll be spending the rest of my life there in the manor of Bernewelle. I know that the whole household from the ale wife to the boy who turns the spit in the kitchen will thoroughly enjoy taking an inordinate interest in the most intimate details of our first night. I know that the ceremony will win the approval of the whole manor — since they were denied the actual wedding — the deflowering of the Lord's new wedded wife — I just wish it was over.'

Emma's husband grasped her wrist in a firm clasp — for her hands were gripping the edge of the sheet. He carried her hand up to his cheek, nuzzling along the line of knuckle and palm with small comforting kisses.

'Afraid of me too — the ravening wolf? Truly you have no cause, I am no clumsy boy.'

Emma shook her head.

In the shadowy light of the last guttering candle Sir Berengar put two fingers under her chin, and tilted her head to look into her eyes, smiling intimately.

'I promise you a gentle wooing — now — a change of tone. Suppose you tell me the real reason why you lie awake?'

He felt her quick intake of breath and chuckled — 'Well?'

Emma began to trace patterns on the coverlet with her finger.

'It is — '

'Yes?'

'It is — '

'I am waiting,' somewhat grimly.

'It is — Diote.'

'Diote.' He sounded thunderstruck.

'But you knew of Diote — you knew she was an episode, long past.'

'Yes,' — somewhat cowed — 'But.'

'But?' The voice had grown impatient.

Emma thought, 'I should certainly have kept quiet, and went on, 'But Diote knew how to give you pleasure — and I do not — and I fear I shall not pleasure you as she did.'

It came out in a rush at the end.

There was silence. Then his hand turned down the sheet and covers for a foot or so, his arm slid round Emma until her head rested against his shoulder.

There was laughter in his voice.

'You think I'll not find pleasure in teaching you to love?'

He bit her ear experimentally. 'Foolish one.'

Strangely comforted, Emma slid her hand up over her husband's cheek and ruffled his hair. He tickled the palm of her hand, then kissed it. 'A promise for Bernewelle,' he murmured against her ear.

20

On August 29th the King proposed to spend the morning riding towards a heronry near the Welland valley, hawking along the banks of a stream on the way.

Short winged goshawks would be used for brook hawking, long winged peregrines for heron hawking.

Four falconers accompanied the King's party. Two falconers held a peregrine each on the gloved fist, two more held a grey goshawk each.

The Lord Edward and his young wife the Lady Eleanor rode near King Henry and Queen Eleanor. About twelve courtiers accompanied the King's party, among them were Sir Berengar and the Lady Emma, there by the invitation of the Lord Edward, after he had gained the King's permission.

As she rode out of Geddington and into Rockingham Forest Emma felt a surge of joyousness. Sir Berengar looked at her with such appreciation in his glance she felt that everything must go well on the morrow, the day that they would leave Geddington and ride to Bernewelle. They would need to travel on August 30th, for the King planned to leave Geddington on the 31st August.

Emma revelled in the intense green of the forest. Many of the oak trees had ivy growing round their trunks, twining up to wreathe round their branches.

Soon the Lord Edward and the Lady Eleanor rode to join Sir Berengar and his new bride.

'Last time we hawked we discussed the trouble that is marring many a joust,' recalled the Lord Edward. He frowned in remembrance. 'Trouble came from the turbulent squires. It was not so much the fault of the knights as of the squires, footmen and spectators who got out of hand. Since then I have planned some provisions which I hope my father will approve of when times are fit. The rules are for regulating behaviour at a tournament.'

Sir Berengar looked quickly at the Lord Edward, opened his mouth to ask the obvious question, then shut it again.

'Very well,' replied the Lord Edward, smiling wryly, 'You shall hear what they are — twelve in all — but in confidence, as my former companion at arms. One, no earl, baron or knight shall have more than three esquires. Two, each of the esquires shall wear the badge of the Lord whom

154

he serves for the day. Three, no knight or squire is to carry pointed sword or knife, or stick or club, but only a broad sword for tourneying. Four, standard bearers are to be armed with defensive armour only — knee caps, thigh pieces, and shoulder pieces of cane. Five, all are to obey the committee — and knights who do not are to lie in prison at the will of the committee, and lose their equipment. Six, squires who do not obey the committee are to lose horse and arms and lie three years in jail. Seven, no one is to assist a fallen knight except his own squires — penalty — three years in jail. Eight, a cadet is only to be armed with knee caps and thigh pieces — on pain of losing the horse he is riding for the day — and three years in jail. Nine, spectators are not to wear any kind of armour and are to be penalized like squires. Ten, no groom or footman is to carry pointed sword, pointed knife, club, stick or stone on pain of lying seven years in jail. Eleven, if any great Lord holds a feast he is not to admit any squires except those who carve for their Lord. Twelve, heralds and marshals are to carry no concealed arms save their blunted swords, and the kings of heralds are to wear their mantles of arms and no more.'

Sir Berengar took a deep breath — 'Whew,

sire, that should keep trouble at bay.'

'I fear that the time for introducing the subject to my father is not opportune as yet, but it will come,' said the Lord Edward.

The track began to dwindle away until the path could hardly be seen.

Suddenly it led into a clearing — no empty glade — but peopled by thirteen men, three carcasses of deer on the grass, and a fantastic sight in the centre of the glade.

All movement ceased as the party reined in and gazed at the stake in the centre of the glade. On it was mounted the head of a buck. In the buck's mouth was placed a spindle. The mouth opened towards the sun in defiance of the King and his foresters.

There was the cracking of a twig and the scene dissolved into movement.

The thirteen men melted discreetly away carrying their bows and arrows with them.

Sir Berengar shrugged. 'Thirteen — a coven of twelve and the leader. Many desolate places cling to the old religion that was here before the coming of the Christian Faith.'

The Lord Edward brought his wife to ride beside Emma. He introduced Emma to the young Lady Eleanor, then left them to ride together while he rode behind with Sir Berengar.

In her prettily accented voice the Lady Eleanor wished Emma joy in her marriage. Blushing, Emma confessed that the bedding would take place at Bernewelle on the morrow.

'You are fortunate to be of suitable age for full marriage,' commented the Lady Eleanor. 'I long to give my husband an heir, but the Queen deems me too young for full marriage as yet — but many girls have given their husbands an heir at thirteen.'

'The time will soon pass,' comforted Emma, 'You will have many children and many happy years with the Lord Edward.'

The two young wives were on excellent terms of friendship by the time the cavalcade reached the side of a brook.

Goshawks could be flown in enclosed country unsuitable for peregrines, even the willow lined bed of a brook.

A goshawk may be slipped at any quarry within range. She will catch it or put it into cover in the first hundred yards, or not at all.

For brook hawking goshawks can be entered at coot, moorhen, mallard — or anything else that moves.

The King and the Lord Edward rode on with a grey short winged goshawk on gloved fist.

Emma hid a smile. Against the light the goshawks ludicrously appeared to be wearing braies, a male undergarment she had often seen pegged to a line, drying, but of which, in her previously unmarried state she was supposed to be ignorant.

Today Emma rode empty handed, a spectator.

As the King, at the head of the group, rode beside the brook he disturbed a pair of mallards — duck and drake, who rose from the water, taking off in a long, flapping ascent along the surface, appearing to tread along the surface of the stream with their limp toes before the strong clapping beat of their wings took them away from the water, leaving it surging out in small waves from their wake.

The King released his goshawk, so did the Lord Edward. Their flight was incredibly swift: they overtook the flying duck and drake, who had only just begun to gain height, struck and brought them down.

The falconers retrieved them.

By the time the party left the brookside the goshawks had accounted for four moorhens, three coot, and the duck and drake.

During the ride through the forest to reach the River Welland, the King and the Lord Edward flew their goshawks at any bird that unwarily appeared.

On arriving at the Welland River valley, King Henry and the Lord Edward handed back their goshawks to two falconers, then took a peregrine each from the gloves of the remaining two falconers.

Soon everyone could see the heronry; the cluster of large, clumsily built, untidy nests apparently perched precariously in the tops of the trees.

The King's party waited some distance away to watch for a heron leaving the nest, light, or coming back laden, to the heronry.

The King was waiting for a heron to appear at a moderate height so that the peregrine, on being hooded off, would have to circle up to get above the heron, an advantage which the heron would always try to prevent by circling higher still.

There was a movement from the trees. A heron was flying out, downwind.

She sailed, legs and claws stretched out in a straight line from her body, her long pointed beak attached to the 's' shape of her head and neck that seemed to rest against her back in flight.

The powerful wings, with a strange, unmistakable movement beat her through the air. The primary feathers along the back edge were serrated. She was a full grown heron, about three feet long.

The King hooded off his peregrine which made instantly at the heron, which in turn rose higher in the air, though still flying quickly on her course.

The peregrine made countless stoops at the heron, whose quickness helped her to avoid them.

The flight was so rapid that the King's party had to ride hard to keep the birds in view at all.

After twenty minutes the peregrine and the heron had circled up so high that they looked like dots in the sky.

The peregrine was able, finally, to strike the heron and bring it to the ground.

It lay on its back — wings outspread raggedly, thin long spindly legs askew, bent at right angles, head outflung along the ground.

A floppy carcass now — no graceful throbbing life.

Once the heron had been dispatched the King led his party towards Rockingham Castle.

Soon they were riding up hill towards the track leading to the castle.

In front loomed the Norman gatehouse with its portcullis. Farther along on the left was the towering circular keep.

After riding beneath the gatehouse arch they entered the bailey. Here they were met by the constable of the castle, who was bowing low to the King.

He conducted the King into the long hall where the high table and two flanking tables were set out ready for a meal.

Pages knelt, holding napkins and bowls of water for the guests to wash their hands.

As the meal was proceeding Sir Berengar drew Emma's attention to a large chest by the wall.

'That is King John's chest,' he said, 'He left it behind on his last journey from here to cross the Wash, when his wagons were overtaken by the inrushing tide. He was very fond of Rockingham and stayed here to hunt every year.'

Once the meal was over King Henry went out with the Constable and the Lord Edward to view the rest of the buildings of the castle. They took a secretary with them to the tall circular keep, along the walls, into the chapel and along the moats.

The secretary jotted down all the comments made by the King.

The Constable looked pleased. He was hoping to receive commands — and money — for some rebuilding.

The Lady Eleanor and Queen Eleanor

went with Emma and Sir Berengar to look at the view over the Welland River towards Uppingham.

When the King had finished his business the cavalcade reformed in the bailey and amidst much bowing set off once more up the hill towards the hamlet of Corby and the homeward journey to Geddington.

The hill at Rockingham was steep. On reaching the top Emma turned to glance back at the castle walls and keep.

The track continued through the forest until it came to the cluster of tofts and the church which was Corby hamlet.

The track then continued towards Stanion. Once clear of the hamlet the King and his son, riding once more with grey goshawk on fist, were ready for more sport on the way to Geddington.

As the King rode into an open glade he startled a young hare, which went speeding across the glade, making for bramble bushes on the other side.

The King quickly cast the hood of his grey goshawk. She flew after the hare instantly, descended and grasped him in her claws.

He attempted to get rid of her by jumping into the air and kicking but she held on to him until a falconer reached him and quickly killed him.

Once through Stanion it seemed only a short time before the cavalcade reached Geddington.

Emma and Sir Berengar went at once to their quarters to make ready to take part in the evening meal and festivities.

Emma wore the tawny coloured gown with yellow embroidery round the neck slit — silently giving thanks to her aunt for remembering her mother's stored away gowns and for suggesting that Emma brought them with her.

By the time Emma and Sir Berengar left the vast hall dusk was falling. They had said their farewells to their friends, both old and new, for there was to be an early start for their journey on the morrow.

As they walked across the demesne towards their quarters above the gatehouse Sir Berengar clasped Emma's hand in his. She felt the gentle pressure of his thumb circling the palm of her hand and the insistent tickle to the centre of her palm.

Little shivers of joyful awareness trickled along her spine.

Going round the corner of the chapel Emma caught her foot in a root and stumbled. Sir Berengar turned and in an instant had an arm round her and had swung her against him.

Emma could feel the sudden tenseness of his grip.

He stood, looking down into her face, breathing fast.

The grip tightened until she was pressed ruthlessly against him.

'God, I want you,' he whispered, and his mouth came down on hers in a kiss so hard she was left shaking.

Her arms slid round his neck and she responded wholeheartedly.

'Tomorrow,' he breathed, 'At Bernewelle, where you will be spending the rest of your life with me.'

Emma buried her face in his shoulder. 'Tomorrow,' she echoed.

21

In the morning Emma woke early. The light was just beginning to show through the cracks in the heavy wooden shutters which were barred across the small window.

As the thin slivers of light grew stronger Emma watched the outlines of the room grow from blackness into dim ghostly shapes — the clothes perch, holding the fluid folds of her gown well above floor level, the falcon perch, no longer occupied by its hooded owner, but with the white splashings of mutes down the wall behind, and on the floor beneath to indicate her previous presence. Well, the falcon would be able to return to her perch today.

For today, the 30th day of August would see Emma leave this haven, balanced between the old world and the new.

She thought of the life ahead — today a blank scroll — but tomorrow? Would a child's face be limned on the scroll by the year's end?

Emma jerked her wandering speculations back to the present.

What to wear for the journey? For her first

appearance at Bernewelle Le Moyne. Emma chose the tawny coloured gown with yellow embroidery round the neck slit.

Sir Berengar had told her that the Lord Edward intended to ride with them for part of the way. He would be accompanied by one of his knights — Sir Otho de Grandison — and a small band of riders.

Hours later as Emma waited with the group in the bailey, waited for the Lord Edward to join them, she could take a long look at Sir Otho de Grandison.

Emma knew that her husband liked him — the newcomer to the comrades of the Lord Edward.

Resolutely she squashed a tiny pang of jealousy.

Men seemed to enjoy an easy camaraderie which was denied to women.

Sir Otho was already deep in anecdotes of skirmishes, gesticulating expressively, while they waited for the Lord Edward.

Suddenly a commanding voice was heard.

The familiar slight stammer attached to the sibilhants told them that the Lord Edward was on his way.

As he stepped through the doorway conversation ceased.

He spoke a few gracious words to the Lady Emma, then to her husband, chaffing him.

He adroitly swung his tall, lithe, muscular figure into the saddle and the journey began.

The cavalcade passed under the stone arch in the centre of the gatehouse, trotted down the slope to the level of the river, but did not cross it by the packhouse bridge.

Instead they took the left hand track through the oak forest to Grafton Underwood, then across to Slipton after which the track joined a well trodden one to Islip.

It was here by the banks of the surging River Nene that the Lord Edward and his protective retinue planned to leave Sir Berengar and his wife.

Across the bridge was Thrapston. And beyond Thrapston, four miles beyond the bridge lay Bernewelle Le Moyne.

A rider had been sent ahead to warn the household of Sir Berengar's arrival, and to bring back an escort of four men.

They were awaiting Sir Berengar at the far side of the bridge, ensuring that the last four miles of the journey would be guarded from surprise by Gerold even if he still cherished hopes of snatching Emma.

After the four Bernewelle men on the further bank of the river had been recognised and saluted, the Lord Edward and his entourage bade Sir Berengar and the Lady Emma 'Farewell' and 'God speed' then turned and followed the Lord Edward back towards the line of forest trees.

Sir Berengar and Emma clattered across the bridge, Waleran, Turold and Segar behind them and four stalwart men from Bernewelle in front.

They all turned to watch the Lord Edward's party ride towards the forest and Geddington.

Trotting quickly out of Thrapston the group began the climb up the slope beyond.

Now Emma rode beside her husband. The track was straight. 'An old Roman road,' he said.

As they emerged from the shelter of the trees, a shaft of sunlight struck straight across their faces.

Emma shut her eyes quickly, then shading them with her hand, peered from between her fingers.

Her husband laughed. 'You look exactly the same as when I first saw you.'

Emma smiled back at him as they rode on companionably. Then puzzlement flickered into life.

Turning to him she said, 'Surely I was standing in the shadow of the main door beside my Aunt Quenilda when you first saw me?'

'No,' he smiled again.

That was the second time, seven days ago on the 23rd day of August.

Emma's eyebrows went up questioningly.

'The first time I saw you, you were coming through the slatted gateway of the dog court, and had to shade your eyes from the bright sun.'

'The chapman? That day? When I was fourteen years old?'

His glance became wickedly intimate.

'Yes, that day. The day you defended an unknown young man against the chapman's censure.'

The scene came back to Emma — the look of horror on the chapman's face as he gazed at the brewhouse door behind her.

'You were hidden in the brewhouse — why?'

'So that I could look at you without being seen. Your mother arranged for you to visit the dog court. During that time I entered the brewhouse and waited for you to come back. I did not bargain for the recital of my own misdeeds from the lips of the chapman — nor for your intervention on my behalf. I peered round the brewhouse door to get another look at you.'

It was still baffling.

Sir Berengar took pity on his wife's look of complete bewilderment.

'When I returned to the Welsh Marches from Bernewelle Le Moyne earlier that year your father had occasion to lecture me. He had the right. He'd once saved my life in battle. I told him of Diote — how she had jumped at the chance of marriage during my absence at the Welsh wars. Your father was most stringent. He deplored my lack of faith in letting one light woman sour my attitude to life and women. I was impatient and accused him of having no knowledge of what he was talking about. So he told me of his first unhappy marriage, then of his second very happy marriage. He spoke of his wife, who had remained steadfast under the most severe pressures — then he spoke of a girl — a child who resembled her mother. I jeered and scoffed, but I was secretly impressed by the advice he gave me, as coming from one who had once been exceedingly unhappy. He advocated, in time, my searching for a wife who I could firstly respect, and the building up together of a life of mutual trust. I sneered, but promptly offered to go and inspect his paragon girl-child, inspired I must confess, mostly by bitterness and a desire to prove him wrong. A message was made the excuse — a message to deliver to the Lady Isolda — the rest you know. I returned to the Welsh Marches and offered for your hand in marriage. Your father accepted my offer — subject to my coming of age and your willingness to wed, when you had had time to get to know me. He thought us well suited.'

Another mile along the track and Emma's thoughts were still of that crucial day so long ago.

Then her husband turned his cavalcade on to a subsidiary track to the right.

It wound round a copse — and then there, ahead, was Bernewelle Le Moyne.

The castle of weathered timber stood upon a mound above the level of a small river.

The river flowed down from the right, dividing the castle heights from the knoll on which stood the church and a few tofts.

The stream made a sharp bend from east to north to flow along the base of the length of the earthwork, then another right angled bend, to turn and flow along the north end of the earthworks, from east to west, and yet another angled bend to flow north again.

Here it was joined by a secondary stream coming from the east so that the waters of both enclosed the piece of land north of the castle earthworks.

Emma knew that many Norman castles were built quickly in the shape of a figure of eight, the earth being thrown into the centre of each adjoining circle by digging out the surrounding ditches and piling the earth into the middle of each circle.

The lower circle formed the bailey, the higher, man-made hill became the motte, on which was built a fortress.

But this motte looked lozenge shaped rather than round.

A weathered timber palisade went round the whole area, at the top of the sloping bank, above the river moat, enclosing the whole area of the raised earthwork of motte and bailey.

A strong timber fortress topped the lozenge shaped motte.

There in the bailey were the timber hall and separate kitchen.

'Bernewelle Le Moyne,' indicated Sir Berengar — 'Built by the first Le Moyne to be here. And there,' he pointed to a rise of ground on the opposite side of the small river, 'There is where I shall build my castle of stone.'

Emma remembered the plan and picture drawn in sand — the rectangular plan of stone walls, the rounded towers of stone at the four corners, the rounded towers on either side of the gatehouse.

The vision faded back to bare earth again.

Emma put out her hand. Sir Berengar

took it in a strong clasp, and raised it to his lips with fingers that were suddenly unsteady.

Emma raised her eyes to his face, to see it tinged with colour under the tan, but her glance fell again before the intent, appraising look in his eyes.

It was her turn to colour.

The horses moved on again.

They took the track which led directly to the castle, leaving the church on its knoll to their right.

By the gatehouse stood a group of people from the hamlet.

As the cavalcade rode through and under the arch, Sir Berengar acknowledged their greetings.

In the bailey more people were gathered in welcome.

Emma stood beside her husband as the horses were being led away. She smiled automatically at the announcement of each name.

'Sir John England, Sir John de Harby, John of Barrow, Ralph Suton, Robert Carbonnel, John Clement, Henry Randolf, Robert Smith, Henry the Clerk, William Attecastel.'

The names rolled on and everything was beginning to assume an air of unreality.

Emma was conducted to the hall, which

showed signs of recent repair to the timbers. She was handed over to the care of a short, busy, brisk dame with a homely, kind face who was named Dame Alda.

Dame Alda did not stop talking for the whole of the way from the hall, up the steps, to the solar.

The dream like quality of the proceedings continued.

First the ritual bath, then the combing of hair, the dressing in a clean silk shift, underdress and the light greenish blue watchet coloured gown.

Then Emma was being conducted back to the hall for the celebratory feast, after which would come the celebratory blessing and bedding.

Enfolded by a ceaseless flow of words from Dame Alda, once more the hall was reached and Emma's hand was taken in Sir Berengar's strong clasp.

Emma blinked at him. He seemed a tall, muscular, long armed, long legged, grey eyed stranger.

The dainties produced so painstakingly by the kitchen cooks were wasted on Emma.

She might just as well have been consuming dry bread.

However, she continued to smile, from her place at the centre of the high table, at the mass of strange faces before her.

All too soon Dame Alda reappeared. Emma's husband rose, and handed her over to Dame Alda's ministrations.

Back in the solar Dame Alda made small comforting clucking noises as she helped Emma to disrobe.

Emma was put between the linen sheets. The covers were drawn up to her chin.

Dame Alda bustled to the door. The message that the bride was ready was relayed to one outside.

Then Emma heard the tread of footsteps, and the room seemed suddenly full of people.

Her gaze found one figure in the group, of the tall grey eyed stranger.

He stood, chatting to the priest, the centre of a group of men.

He was wearing a long, handsome bed robe, trimmed by a double row of fur down the front edges and round the borders of the long sleeves.

He suddenly laughed at something that one of the men had quipped, but his eyes remained inscrutable.

He approached the bed. The sheets and covers at that side were drawn back.

Untying the row of bow knots which held the edges of the bed robe together he adroitly slipped between the sheets, discarding the bed robe as he slid down the bed beside Emma.

At a word from the priest this naked muscular stranger took Emma's left hand in his right hand and the blessing began.

Emma had no recollection of what was said. Only waves of sound reached her ears.

Her consciousness was of the strong fingers holding hers, of an inscrutable face beyond her naked shoulder.

The voice ceased. There was laughter, more good wishes, the tread of feet towards the doorway, then through it, Dame Alda's being the last of them. She closed the door behind her — and they were alone.

Her husband made no movement other than to continue to hold Emma's left hand firmly in his right hand.

He was absently regarding it. Then he transferred his grasp to his left hand and began to fiddle with the gold wedding ring, moving it idly up and down her finger.

Emma watched the candlelight catching the oblique decorative curves of the broad band.

The gold had been twisted by the goldsmith into a pattern, almost all the way round, leaving one centre unadorned facet.

Shaken and unsure of herself she felt panic rising — would he never speak?

Then the symbolic significance of the ring upon the finger suddenly hit Emma.

She gasped and tensed, tried to turn away, found her husband's right arm suddenly round her shoulders, holding her so that she could not turn that way, then perforce she turned inwards and buried her face against his shoulder.

His mouth nuzzled her hair. He simply held her tight, apostrophising gently.

The panic began to subside. He began to stroke Emma's hair soothingly, then put his fingers under her chin and forced her to look at him.

The grey eyes were amused and understanding.

'Kyndel,' he whispered, suddenly hoarse, and bent and kissed her, not gently at all but hard, his arms holding her in an intense grip.

The feel of his naked skin against hers was suddenly joy.

She slid her hands to his shoulders and gripped him convulsively. He gasped and let his weight carry them back against the pillows.

His hands began to slide delicately over her body, over the arms, and to cup the breasts, over the tight flat muscle between the hip bones.

His touch awakened Emma to an intensity of longing she hadn't known existed, until she was shuddering with delight, locked against the rhythmic contractions of his body.

Berengar raised himself and leaned over his wife, propping his weight on his hands, one on either side of her shoulders.

Emma lay on her back looking up at him. His head and shoulders blocked out the rafters against the candlelight.

Her husband's eyes were anxiously searching Emma's face.

He asked a question.

A smile began to curl the corners of her mouth.

The answer was only too obvious.

He filled her world.

Glossary

alaunt — ferocious hound — muzzled when not at work.

bailey — the outer court of a castle.

bordar — a villein who held his hut at his lord's pleasure.

chapman — pedlar.

dortoir — a monastic dormitory.

demesne — a manor house or castle with lands adjacent to it.

garde — robe — privy or latrine.

genuflect — bow the knee, especially in worship.

jess — a short, leather strap round the leg of a hawk.

knight service — tenure by a knight on condition of military service.

lymer — scenting hound.

lymerer — a man in charge of a lymer.

manumission — setting free from bondage.

pentice — a lean to projecting from a main building.

rache — beagle type of running hound.

solar — upper chamber, especially for the private use of the family.

subtlety — a figure, building or scene made

of sugar and paste to adorn a banquet.

tiercel peregrine — male falcon — long winged hawk.

toft — homestead.

trace — footprint of a deer.

villein — free in relation to all but his lord.

whelp — puppy.

or — gold.

argent — silver.

gules — red.

azure — blue.

sable — black.

vert — green.

purpure — purple

Short Bibliography

Studies in Medieval History, presented to Sir Frederick Maurice Powicke and edited by R. W. Hunt, W. A. Pantin, R. W. Southern, — by permission of Oxford University Press 1948 — with reference to the chapter, *The Tournament in the Thirteenth Century*, by N. Denholm-Young.

Harting's Hints on the Management of Hawks, and Practical Falconry, by James Edmund Harting.

They looked like this, by Grant Uden.

Life and Times of Edward I, by John Chancellor.

Historical Dances, by Melusine Wood.

Sir Otho de Grandison, by Charles L. Kingsford.

The Victoria County Histories,

The Northamptonshire Landscape, by John M. Steane.

The Reign of Chivalry, by Richard Barber.

Sir Otho de Grandison 1238? – 1328 — Royal Historical Society Transactions, Third Series Vol. 111

Other titles in the
Ulverscroft Large Print Series:

THE GREENWAY
Jane Adams

When Cassie and her twelve-year-old cousin Suzie had taken a short cut through an ancient Norfolk pathway, Suzie had simply vanished . . . Twenty years on, Cassie is still tormented by nightmares. She returns to Norfolk, determined to solve the mystery.

FORTY YEARS
ON THE WILD FRONTIER
Carl Breihan & W. Montgomery

Noted Western historian Carl Breihan has culled from the handwritten diaries of John Montgomery, grandfather of co-author Wayne Montgomery, new facts about Wyatt Earp, Doc Holliday, Bat Masterson and other famous and infamous men and women who gained notoriety when the Western Frontier was opened up.

TAKE NOW, PAY LATER
Joanna Dessau

This fiction based on fact is the love-turning-to-hate story of Robert Carr, Earl of Somerset, and his wife, Frances.

McLEAN AT THE GOLDEN OWL
George Goodchild

Inspector McLean has resigned from Scotland Yard's CID and has opened an office in Wimpole Street. With the help of his able assistant, Tiny, he solves many crimes, including those of kidnapping, murder and poisoning.

KATE WEATHERBY
Anne Goring

Derbyshire, 1849: The Hunter family are the arrogant, powerful masters of Clough Grange. Their feuds are sparked by a generation of guilt, despair and ill-fortune. But their passions are awakened by the arrival of nineteen-year-old Kate Weatherby.

A VENETIAN RECKONING
Donna Leon

When the body of a prominent international lawyer is found in the carriage of an intercity train, Commissario Guido Brunetti begins to dig deeper into the secret lives of the once great and good.

A TASTE FOR DEATH
Peter O'Donnell

Modesty Blaise and Willie Garvin take on impossible odds in the shape of Simon Delicata, the man with a taste for death, and Swordmaster, Wenczel, in a terrifying duel. Finally, in the Sahara desert, the intrepid pair must summon every killing skill to survive.

SEVEN DAYS FROM MIDNIGHT
Rona Randall

In the Comet Theatre, London, seven people have good reason for wanting beautiful Maxine Culver out of the way. Each one has reason to fear her blackmail. But whose shadow is it that lurks in the wings, waiting to silence her once and for all?

QUEEN OF THE ELEPHANTS
Mark Shand

Mark Shand knows about the ways of elephants, but he is no match for the tiny Parbati Barua, the daughter of India's greatest expert on the Asian elephant, the late Prince of Gauripur, who taught her everything. Shand sought out Parbati to take part in a film about the plight of the wild herds today in north-east India.

THE DARKENING LEAF
Caroline Stickland

On storm-tossed Chesil Bank in 1847, the young lovers, Philobeth and Frederick, prevent wreckers mutilating the apparent corpse of a young woman. Discovering she is still alive, Frederick takes her to his grandmother's home. But the rescue is to have violent and far-reaching effects . . .

A WOMAN'S TOUCH
Emma Stirling

When Fenn went to stay on her uncle's farm in Africa, the lovely Helena Starr seemed to resent her — especially when Dr Jason Kemp agreed to Fenn helping in his bush hospital. Though it seemed Jason saw Fenn as little more than a child, her feelings for him were those of a woman.

A DEAD GIVEAWAY
Various Authors

This book offers the perfect opportunity to sample the skills of five of the finest writers of crime fiction — Clare Curzon, Gillian Linscott, Peter Lovesey, Dorothy Simpson and Margaret Yorke.

DOUBLE INDEMNITY — MURDER FOR INSURANCE
Jad Adams

This is a collection of true cases of murderers who insured their victims then killed them — or attempted to. Each tense, compelling account tells a story of cold-blooded plotting and elaborate deception.

THE PEARLS OF COROMANDEL
By Keron Bhattacharya

John Sugden, an ambitious young Oxford graduate, joins the Indian Civil Service in the early 1920s and goes to uphold the British Raj. But he falls in love with a young Hindu girl and finds his loyalties tragically divided.

WHITE HARVEST
Louis Charbonneau

Kathy McNeely, a marine biologist, sets out for Alaska to carry out important research. But when she stumbles upon an illegal ivory poaching operation that is threatening the world's walrus population, she soon realises that she will have to survive more than the harsh elements . . .

TO THE GARDEN ALONE
Eve Ebbett

Widow Frances Morley's short, happy marriage was childless, and in a succession of borders she attempts to build a substitute relationship for the husband and family she does not have. Over all hovers the shadow of the man who terrorized her childhood.

CONTRASTS
Rowan Edwards

Julia had her life beautifully planned — she was building a thriving pottery business as well as sharing her home with her friend Pippa, and having fun owning a goat. But the goat's problems brought the new local vet, Sebastian Trent, into their lives.

MY OLD MAN AND THE SEA
David and Daniel Hays

Some fathers and sons go fishing together. David and Daniel Hays decided to sail a tiny boat seventeen thousand miles to the bottom of the world and back. Together, they weave a story of travel, adventure, and difficult, sometimes terrifying, sailing.

SQUEAKY CLEAN
James Pattinson

An important attribute of a prospective candidate for the United States presidency is not to have any dirt in your background which an eager muckraker can dig up. Senator William S. Gallicauder appeared to fit the bill perfectly. But then a skeleton came rattling out of an English cupboard.

NIGHT MOVES
Alan Scholefield

It was the first case that Macrae and Silver had worked on together. Malcolm Underdown had brutally stabbed to death Edward Craig and had attempted to murder Craig's fiancée, Jane Harrison. He swore he would be back for her. Now, four years later, he has simply walked from the mental hospital. Macrae and Silver must get to him — before he gets to Jane.

GREATEST CAT STORIES
Various Authors

Each story in this collection is chosen to show the cat at its best. James Herriot relates a tale about two of his cats. Stella Whitelaw has written a very funny story about a lion. Other stories provide examples of courageous, clever and lucky cats.

THE HAND OF DEATH
Margaret Yorke

The woman had been raped and murdered. As the police pursue their relentless inquiries, decent, gentle George Fortescue, the typical man-next-door, finds himself accused. While the real killer serenely selects his third victim — and then his fourth . . .

VOW OF FIDELITY
Veronica Black

Sister Joan of the Daughters of Compassion is shocked to discover that three of her former fellow art college students have recently died violently. When another death occurs, Sister Joan realizes that she must pit her wits against a cunning and ruthless killer.

MARY'S CHILD
Irene Carr

Penniless and desperate, Chrissie struggles to support herself as the Victorian years give way to the First World War. Her childhood friends, Ted and Frank, fall hopelessly in love with her. But there is only one man Chrissie loves, and fate and one man bent on revenge are determined to prevent the match . . .

THE SWIFTEST EAGLE
Alice Dwyer-Joyce

This book moves from Scotland to Malaya — before British Raj and now — and then to war-torn Vietnam and Cambodia . . . Virginia meets Gareth casually in the Western Isles, with no inkling of the sacrifice he must make for her.

VICTORIA & ALBERT
Richard Hough

Victoria and Albert had nine children and the family became the archetype of the nineteenth century. But the relationship between the Queen and her Prince Consort was passionate and turbulent; thunderous rows threatened to tear them apart, but always reconciliation and love broke through.

BREEZE: WAIF OF THE WILD
Marie Kelly

Bernard and Marie Kelly swapped their lives in London for a remote farmhouse in Cumbria. But they were to undergo an even more drastic upheaval when a two-day-old fragile roe deer fawn arrived on their doorstep. The knowledge of how to care for her was learned through sleepless nights and anxiety-filled days.

DEAR LAURA
Jean Stubbs
In Victorian London, Mr Theodore Crozier, of Crozier's Toys, succumbed to three grains of morphine. Wimbledon hoped it was suicide — but murder was whispered. Out of the neat cupboards of the Croziers' respectable home tumbled skeleton after skeleton.

MOTHER LOVE
Judith Henry Wall
Karen Billingsly begins to suspect that her son, Chad, has done something unthinkable — something beyond her wildest fears or imaginings. Gradually the terrible truth unfolds, and Karen must decide just how far she should go to protect her son from justice.

JOURNEY TO GUYANA
Margaret Bacon
In celebration of the anniversary of the emancipation of the African slaves in Guyana, the author published an account of her two-year stay there in the 1960s, revealing some fascinating insights into the multi-racial society.

WEDDING NIGHT
Gary Devon

Young actress Callie McKenna believes that Malcolm Rhodes is the man of her dreams. But a dark secret long buried in Malcolm's past is about to turn Callie's passion into terror.

RALPH EDWARDS
OF LONESOME LAKE
Ed Gould

Best known for his almost single-handed rescue of the trumpeter swans from extinction in North America, Ralph Edwards relates other aspects of his long, varied life, including experiences with his missionary parents in India, as a telegraph operator in World War I, and his eventual return to Lonesome Lake.

NEVER FAR FROM NOWHERE
Andrea Levy

Olive and Vivien were born in London to Jamaican parents. Vivien's life becomes a chaotic mix of friendships, youth clubs, skinhead violence, discos and college. But Olive, three years older and her skin a shade darker, has a very different tale to tell . . .

THE UNICORN SUMMER
Rhona Martin

When Joanna Pengerran was a child, she escaped from her murderous stepfather and took refuge among the tinkers. Across her path blunders Angel, a fugitive from prejudice and superstition. It is a meeting destined to disrupt both their lives.

FAMILY REUNIONS
Connie Monk

Claudia and Teddy's three children are now married, and it is a time to draw closer together again, man and wife rather than mother and father. But then their daughter introduces Adrian into the family circle. Young and attractive, Adrian arouses excitement and passion in Claudia that she had never expected to feel again.

SHADOW OF THE MARY CELESTE
Richard Rees

In 1872, the sailing ship *Mary Celeste* left New York. Exactly one month later, she was found abandoned — but completely seaworthy — six hundred miles off the coast of Spain, with no sign of captain or crew. After years of exhaustive research Richard Rees has unravelled the mystery.

PINKMOUNT DRIVE
Jan Webster

Twelve years ago, moving into the splendid new houses of Pinkmount Drive, they had thought the good times would go on forever. Then came the recession that would take its toll on all their lives.

EMMA WATSON
Joan Aiken

It has always been a source of great frustration to Janeites that Jane Austen abandoned THE WATSONS after only seventeen and a half thousand words. Here, Joan Aitken has used Austen's characters, but has made them her own.

THE MAKING OF MOLLY MARCH
Juliet Dymoke

Life is never easy for a workhouse girl, and Molly's is no exception. Yet fate has wider horizons in store for her. Molly finds herself following the drum in the Crimea, where her indomitable courage wins the reluctant admiration of Captain Matthew Hamilton.

WITH MY SOUL AMONGST LIONS
Gareth Patterson

When George Adamson was murdered, Gareth Patterson vowed to continue his work. He successfully cared for and restored George's lion cubs, who were once again orphaned, into the wild. Batian, Furaha and Rafiki became his life's work and he became one of their pride.

FIELDS OF LIGHT
Jim Rickards

In 1931, Brian Grover sought fortune and adventure in Stalin's murderously dangerous Soviet Union. In Moscow, he met beautiful Ileana Petrovna, and they began an extraordinary love affair that was to enchant the world. This is the true story of Brian Grover's courage, bravery and unswerving determination to be with the woman he loved.

THE LAST TIME I SAW MOTHER
Arlene J. Chai

Caridad is a wife and mother, a native of the Philippines living in Australia. Out of the blue, Caridad's mother summons her home to reveal a secret that has been weighing heavily upon her for years. So begins Caridad's journey of discovery as she is given the gift of her past.

RETURN TO MOONDANCE
Anne Goring

Miranda enjoys a carefree childhood at Moondance, an old house on the edge of Dartmoor. When she is orphaned at the age of ten, Moondance's new owner arranges for her to work at a Derbyshire cotton mill, where conditions are harsh and pitiless. Miranda dreams of taking revenge on the man who ruined her childhood — but will she choose revenge over true love?

CALEB'S KINGDOM
Essie Summers

After her fiancé's death, Greta feels she must have a complete change. She hears that a sheep farm in New Zealand's Lake District needs help while its owner, Caleb Armstrong is away in Europe. The spectacular surroundings work their magic on Greta, but the return of Caleb Armstrong ends her new-found peace of mind. For her attraction to him is far too disturbing for comfort . . .